S0-BNV-661

THE BAND OF GYPSIES

A Novel

by

Enrico Antiporda

Enjoy the book!
—Enrico

Blue Owl Editions
Oakland, CA

Publication Date: 2000

Copyright © 1999 Enrico Antiporda

All rights reserved. No part of this book may be reproduced or transmitted in any form or by any means, electronic, mechanical, including photocopying, recording, or by any information storage and retrieval system, without the written permission from the Publisher except when permitted by law.

This is a work of fiction. In no way does it intend to represent any real event or person, living or dead.

First Edition
10 9 8 7 6 5 4 3 2 1

ISBN 0-9672793-0-5
Library of Congress Catalogue Number: 99-90592

Acknowledgement

Many thanks to my Rockridge Writers Group: Joel Brooks, Allison Alsup, Christine Acker, Jim Street, Jack Hawk, Carolyn Brown, Dick Heister, Loretta Sheridan, and Patrick Healy for the painful but invaluable critique. Thanks also to Michele Baack for the structural input and my SBWC painter/writer friend Sue Mendes for feedback on the artwork and jacket text. I would like to thank my friends and flatmates in Bilbao: Knut, Krister, Iñigo, Jose Luis, Jorge, Maite, Chelo, Maribel, and her mother Señora Morquillas, and the three who traveled south with me: Txeli, Annie, and Annabel for the magical experiences. Most of all, thanks to my wife and best friend Sandy who never stopped believing; I could never have written this novel without her.

Cover Art & Design by Enrico Antiporda © 1999
Front Cover: Gypsy Dancers; Back Cover: The Bullring

Printed in the U.S.A.

Published by:

Blue Owl Editions
(510) 482-3038; Email: blueowl@jps.net

See back pages for excerpts of the sequel IBERIAN NIGHTS

For Sandy

PROLOGUE

We were huddled in my uncle's vacation home, a bamboo slat house with thatched roof overlooking Manila Bay. My uncle Lauro had joined us for the private meeting as had my first cousin Bartello, a military captain who would smuggle me through the airport for my flight to Spain.

"I can't do this," I said, holding back tears.

"You know you have to, Jaime," my father said. "They'll never leave you alone."

"But what about Marina? I can't just..."

My father chopped the air impatiently. "I know how close you two are. But there is nothing you can do for her. Your sister is convalescing in a convent. The important thing is for you to get out now."

I turned to Bartello who nodded in agreement. "Your father is right Jaime. Your life is in grave danger here. Already, I heard rumors that General Sanchez has sent out his thugs for you. We don't have much time."

I shook my head bitterly. "His son rapes my sister and I'm the one being punished."

"No one is blaming you, Jaime," Bartello said. "You were right to defend your sister. I would've done the same thing. But his son Pancho is in serious condition. That's all that matters to him." Bartello put a hand on my shoulder. "He can't win in court, Jaime. He knows that. But believe me, he'll try to get you another way."

I trudged over to the window. The sun was setting, a glowing ball of orange hovering over the flickering bay. I could see the fishnets in the water held up by bamboo poles, the grass houses on stilts that served as guardhouses. Pig pens at sea, I used to call them.

I took a deep breath and smelled the salt air redolent of fish and dried seaweed. Not long ago, I used these private moments to fantasize about my coming internship in Spain, a country I had longed to see. It was a yearning dating back to my childhood when my great grandfather, a transplanted Spaniard, would put me on his lap and tell me vivid tales about Andalusia and its scorching landscape, and always, he would recount those stories with a sense of magic. I remembered listening to him for hours, hanging on to his every word.

I loved the Castilian sunsets he conveyed, the gypsy wails he mimicked, I loved the Moorish castles he described complete with turrets and parapets. Most of all, I loved the Spanish women he portrayed, those dark-haired tempests whose seething passion was enough to rouse the dead. I had always pictured them with fiery eyes, dominant noses, blood red lips that curled sensually into a sneer. But now, that dream was gone. Somehow, it didn't seem important anymore.

The Band Of Gypsies

"Time to go, Jaime," Bartello said.

I looked at him and nodded. His left eye twitched. I knew he was concerned; so many things could go wrong at the airport, so many unforeseen events.

"Go see your mother," my father said, nodding towards the den where she was packing a suitcase. She was still wearing that wrinkled summer dress she had snatched from the closet when they hustled me out of the house in haste. Her legs were bare as were her feet. Despite a touch of gray hair creeping up on her temples, she was still the most beautiful woman I had ever seen. "Mama," I said.

She pretended to be busy with the suitcase, trying to zip it close.

"Stay out of trouble in Spain, Jaime," she said, pushing away her tears. "Start a new life there. It is what your sister would want." She reminded me that life in Spain would be different, that everyone would be a stranger. *"You'll be all alone. If something happens, you'll have no one to turn to."*

I took her in my arms. "Don't worry, Mama. I'll be okay." At the time, I was unaware of the prophetic significance of her words. In a way, I was scared. I had never been out of the country; never been with anyone but my own kind.

A footstep sounded behind me. "We better go, Jaime," Bartello said from the door. I noticed he had strapped on his Browning and was cradling an Armalite rifle in the crook of his arm. "Colonel Villegas just called from the airport. Everything is set."

☼ 1 Bilbao, Spain
The Exile

They assassinated the Governor the day I flew into town. They did it with a car bomb planted across the street from his house. It not only killed him, but also his wife, his dog, his two kids, and the maids. It was with this atmosphere of siege that I descended upon the tarmac in Bilbao greeted by a surge of anxious faces. Everywhere I turned, I saw armed guards.

A bearded man shouldered through the crowd. "Are you Miguel Ruiz?" he demanded in English, pronouncing Ruiz with a lot of rolling R's.

"No, I'm Jaime Aragon," I said haltingly. "From Manila."

I didn't understand it then but I guess he and his tall friend had mistaken me for another intern arriving from Venezuela. I tried to explain who I was, but they waved it off, took my bags, and hustled me off to a waiting sedan. I knew something was afoot the minute we stepped out of the terminal, for I saw men in combat fatigues scrambling around the loading zones. A profusion of blue lights was flashing. Someone bellowed orders through a megaphone.

"We better get out of here," the bearded Spaniard said, frowning at the chaos. "I do not like the looks of this." He yanked the car door open and ushered me in. "Listo?" he asked his lanky friend.

"Si," the tall man answered. An armored truck rumbled by and stopped fifty feet away, turret swiveling.

Cautiously, we pulled away from the curb, swung into the driving lane, and coasted along the police cordon. No one spoke. More armored trucks rolled in. It was only when we had gone a mile completely out of view of the airport that the bearded man looked at me through the rearview mirror. "I'm Jose Mari, president of the training program." He nodded to his lanky companion. "And this is Iñaki, your reception officer."

"What was that all about?" I asked Iñaki who had turned from the passenger seat to shake my hand. It was the first time I noticed his face; bony, hollow, fronted by a toothy grin.

"They assassinated the Governor today. Car bomb in an auto," Iñaki said in accented English. "His entire family, boom!" He threw up his hands. But he added, "Ah, but not to worry, amigo. This is routine, si? Bombs go off all the time in Bilbao."

Great, I thought. I wondered what other surprises awaited me in this great city.

"You do not have terrorists in Manila, yes?"

"No. No terrorists. Just private armies who fight all the time."

"Private army? What is that?"

"Oh, they're these thugs hired by politicians. Sometimes they get into fights during the election and throw grenades at each other."

Iñaki gave me a funny look but didn't say anything.

We lapsed into silence, lost in our own thoughts and it was only when we were well on our way to Bilbao that Jose Mari spoke again, this time in Spanish. "Estas muy temprano, eh. You are too early. Your traineeship doesn't start for four weeks." He shook his head. "You took a big chance. We haven't even received the contract from the company." He had to repeat himself a few times before I understood.

"Ah si, si. I—I thought I'd explore the city first." Something clawed in my belly. *Get a grip,* I told myself. *Don't let it get to you. It'll be hard enough as it is.*

It was at this point that my preoccupations were quickly forgotten, replaced by a more immediate one, for Jose Mari was now driving like a maniac, careening down the hill at eighty kilometers per hour, hardly slowing down for the hairpin turns. I grabbed the armrest in panic while Iñaki, seated in front, thought nothing of his friend's acrobatic driving.

We raced down a long series of switchbacks and soon, metropolitan Bilbao came into view with its collection of towering smokestacks. I gave a sigh of disappointment as I wondered what I had gotten myself into. I expected a quaint European city with stately ornate buildings and winding canals, what I found was an industrial metropolis crowded with factories billowing black soot into the red sunset. A mocha-colored river stretched out for miles, cutting through the city like a Moorish scimitar. All along the riverbank were giant cranes, some as high as eight and nine stories under which were ships in various stages of manufacture. We had to stop for ten minutes because the Deusto Bridge had separated to let a cargo ship pass through.

"Esta es la Puente de Deusto. That's the Deusto Bridge. One of the longest in Spain," Jose Mari said proudly.

"Your apartment is on the other side of Bilbao overlooking the university," Iñaki joined in, sweeping an arm across the city. "Beautiful, eh?"

I nodded, too anesthetized to respond.

The much-touted apartment building was passable, a weather-stained four story structure on a hill adjacent to the manicured lawns of Universidad De Deusto. I noticed the pockmarks on its walls, as if someone had let loose on it with an automatic.

"Don't worry about those," Iñaki said nonchalantly.

The building's owner, Doña Moncha, was a matronly woman of about forty-five with dyed-blond hair, black roots showing, and a winning smile. "Ven, ven," she said as she waddled through a boxy lobby, past a row of mailboxes, into a stairwell that had little light. I was caught in the moment.

I was supposed to be on the fourth floor but there were no elevators in the building, so we trotted up the rickety stairway barely wide enough to accommodate the Señora. Its walls were so old I could see the uneven surface of the plaster, the festoons of peeling paint, and brown blotches of stain where the heavy Bilbao rains had seeped through the cracks in the wall. After much grunting and wheezing on the Señora's part, we reached my floor, thank God, for I thought she was about to have a coronary.

"Esto es tu yo. This is your apartment," she said, unlocking the door. She handed me the key.

We entered a flat with a long hallway wallpapered in paisley, accented by a disturbing Goya poster depicting men being executed by firing squad. "Goya," the Señora volunteered without my asking. She pointed an arm through the dark corridor, two fingers extended, as though directing traffic at the Gran Via. "Straight ahead," she announced whereupon she marched us into the first bedroom on the right, a twelve by fifteen foot cell containing a desk, a battered oak armoire, and two twin beds with plaid bedspreads. A blond man was stretched out on one of them reading a Viking comic book. He looked up and smiled with bloodshot eyes.

"This is your roommate Bjorn Brondheim, from Sweden," Doña Moncha declared.

"Hola," the guy said haltingly. Why did I have the distinct feeling that that was the only Spanish word he knew? But I shrugged it off and parried with an "Hola" of my own.

A young woman came to the door yawning sleepily. Dressed only in a long tee shirt, she had the most golden skin I had ever seen. It glowed, much like a copper utensil in a ray of light.

"Por Dios, what's all this noise?" she asked. She rubbed her eyes and stretched. Nipples jutted against the thin material. I pulled my gaze away.

"Your new roommate has arrived," the Señora exclaimed. "Jaime, I'd like you to meet Elena. From Brazil."

Elena smiled. "Bienvenido. Welcome to Bilbao." She jerked a thumb at the partition wall. "I am right next door.

But not to worry. Except for the radio, I do not make a lot of noise."

"Y Allison. Donde esta?" the Señora asked.

Elena rolled her eyes. "Ay Señora. You should know by now. She's on a date. She said she's going to be a little late."

"Again? With whom?" the Señora demanded.

"With this guy *Francisco*. You know, he's a—"

"I know who he is," the Señora cut in. She shook her head in disgust. "She does nothing but date. She should concentrate on her studies if you ask me." With that, the Señora whipped around and left.

I looked at Bjorn and Elena who shrugged at the Señora's sudden outburst. Welcome to Bilbao, I thought.

☼2 Bloodshed At The Plaza

"Jaime, wake up!" Dona Moncha admonished. "Por dios. It's already ten."

"Oh Moncha, can I have a few more minutes?" I begged, groaning in bed.

"Ay que gambero." She took Bjorn's pillow and bashed me over the head with it. I sat up dazedly and mumbled a protest to the juvenile giggles of her nieces.

"Bueno, bueno, I'm up, I'm up."

Two weeks had passed and I had sunk into a brooding mood. The uncertainty of my traineeship had begun to nag on me. I couldn't eat, I couldn't sleep, each night in my room became a battle with the bed sheets. It was during these moments of self-doubt that I became terribly homesick. I missed my friends, my family. Twice, I went through the exercise of packing my bags only to dejectedly concede defeat. The reality was, I couldn't go home. Anyway, I had never been a quitter.

Dona Moncha's constant ravings became a morning ritual. Each day at ten, she would barge into my room and forcibly eject me from bed so she could clean it. And always, her teenage nieces would be with her and a hired maid named Maricarmen who was working the menial job of house cleaning to put herself through college.

Maricarmen, at eighteen, was an eyeful: long sweeps of raven hair, dark midnight eyes, and a sharp thin nose that sometimes made her look prim but did not detract in any way from her classic Iberian beauty. She often gave me oblique glances while cleaning my room such that I began to have wild fantasies about her; Maricarmen dusting the window in the buff, Maricarmen naked in bed with her legs spread wide, Maricarmen playing with herself. Testosterone levels surged, filthy musings surfaced in my mind.

One day, Maricarmen caught me with a morning erection as I got out of bed and quipped, "Que es eso?" pointing at the puptent. To my abject embarrassment, the girls burst out laughing, pitifully deflating my manhood. Thank God Dona Moncha had been there to chase them out of the room or I wouldn't have been able to endure their ridicule.

"You're too shy, Jaime," the Señora commented. "You're just like that Filipino intern who stayed here last year. A silent type. Kept to himself a lot."

I nodded, knowing exactly how the man felt. "Filipinos are a shy people, Señora. I guess it came with all those years of being colonized," I said as an easy explanation.

The Señora looked at me thoughtfully. "Yes...maybe so. But you're different, Jaime. Much different from any boarder

I've had." She narrowed her eyes. "There's something about you."

I crunched an eyebrow.

"You're interesting, Jaime," she explained. "When you first walked in that door, I didn't know what to make of you. You looked South American, but you also looked Asian. African even. And you have this glow...this presence...like a silent mountain."

I shrugged away the comment. The lineage on my father's side had never been clear. My third great-grandfather was rumored to have been an Italian actor who entertained the royal household in Madrid before coming to the Philippines with the ruling governor of the colony. I was supposed to be the product of several generations of intermarriages of which included a Chinese merchant, an Indian trader from New Delhi, a renegade pirate from Borneo, and a long line of Spanish Civil Guards, among others. Of course, I didn't know how much of it was concocted by my grandfather who had a habit of changing his story every so often to suit his mood.

With everyone off at work, the Señora and Maricarmen became my daytime companions and I could never thank them enough for what they had done for me. They not only taught me the subtleties of the Spanish language, but gave me lessons about Bilbao, the Basques or Vascos as they liked to be called, and their customs which somewhat prepared me for the violence that would later manifest itself.

As if to prove this point, I accompanied the Señora and Maricarmen to the Bilbao Marketplace; it was to be my first glimpse of the volatile situation in the Vascongadas. We had boarded the 14 Marquina bus to downtown Bilbao and were walking down a main thoroughfare towards Casco Viejo when we came upon a caravan of gray vans parked along Avenida Torino. There must have been fifty of them with turreted tops and cabins shaped like armored trucks. I asked Dona Moncha about them and she whispered, "La Guardia Civil. Muy mal, eh. Very bad." She shook a stubby finger.

A shiver coursed through me. The Guardia Civil. I had heard about them. The Spanish version of the special police, they had the reputation of being ruthless enforcers for the Madrid government. I scanned the street uneasily, but didn't find them anywhere. I did sense a certain edginess in the pedestrians. It showed in the way they walked, the way they scurried along the sidewalk flinging nervous glances behind them, and as we drew nearer the plaza which we must walk across to reach the marketplace, I heard the loud chanting of many people. The Señora and Maricarmen had picked up the pace, and I hurried to catch up.

We turned the corner and there they were; throngs and throngs of them, at least ten thousand strong, waving placards and Basque flags, taunting the police with chants of disdain. Across the plaza directly facing the mob stood the stone-faced Guardia Civil gripping short-barreled machine pistols. They wore gray uniforms and three-cornered black hats with flat tops and pointed brims, not unlike a Dutch boy's hat, only black and shiny which made them look grim. Some wore riot gear complete with facemasks, shields, and batons.

The crowd's chants rose in volume and it was only then that I became aware that they weren't chanting in Spanish but rather in a foreign tongue the likes of which I had never heard before. A bottle hurtled over the crowd and shattered in front of the Guardia Civil. Another one smashed into a guard's shield, knocking him back.

"Asca naciona gora euzkadi askatuta," the crowd screamed.

I asked Dona Moncha what was going on and she said, "Manifestaciones. It's the second year anniversary of the massacre at San Sebastian." Apparently thirty Basque demonstrators were killed in that rally when the Guardia Civil open-fired into the crowd with live ammunition.

There was an explosive tension in the air. I could smell it, almost even touch it. The demonstrators swelled forward, threatening the Guardia Civil, who tensed and lifted their assault rifles. I cringed.

"Ay, come on, walk faster. No time to snoop," Dona Moncha admonished. We had just crossed the plaza and turned the corner to the marketplace when it happened. Dona Moncha was already far ahead of us, but Maricarmen and I stopped to watch.

It started with a pop, promptly followed by a deafening boom. Someone screamed, more agitated shouts, then pandemonium broke loose. The crowd surged forward and the Guardia Civil retreated taking on a defensive stance. Rocks and bottles hurtled at the guards, pounding their shields with shards of glass. Molotov cocktails exploded sending ribbons of black smoke up the air. A long volley of shots followed. Brrrt! Brrrt! Brrrt! I saw a man fall, then another. A display window shattered behind us.

Oh my God, they're killing them, I thought. A man staggered by, clutching a bloody chest. At once, the plaza was filled with screaming people, running in every direction. Smoke and tear gas filled the air.

The Band Of Gypsies

I grabbed Maricarmen's hand and dragged her through the stalls trying to catch up with Dona Moncha, who had already made it on the other side of the marketplace.

"Ven, ven," Dona Moncha called out as more pops erupted from the alley.

She led us out of the tented marketplace, across a bridge with a gentle arch, down a flight of stairs into a secluded underpass bus stop. She stood gasping for air, wheezing heavily. When Maricarmen and I caught up with her, she said, "Que horor! We must now go to the market in Baracaldo. It is the only place I can find good *callos* for dinner." Later that day, I found out that her precious callos was nothing more than a slab of tripe in garlic gelatin.

That night, I had a dream. I dreamt General Sanchez swept into town in an armored caravan. Except he didn't look like a Filipino general anymore. He was wearing a gray uniform and a three-cornered black hat. He had a determined look about him: lips tight, eyes glinting, eyebrows bushed together at the bridge. Behind him, cloaked under the shadows was a man. A familiar looking man.

The caravan stopped in front of the apartment building and everyone got out. The street light hit the stranger's face. My breath caught. My God, it's Pancho Sanchez, his face as torn up as the night I left him. Awestruck, I gazed down at the ghostly scene and watched the Señora and Maricarmen emerge from the house. They spoke to the General in whispered tones. Suddenly, I became angry. Very angry. How could they betray me? I thought they were my friends. But then, the General pulled out a gun. It went off and the Señora staggered back clutching her bosom. More shots rang out. I saw the Señora fall, then Maricarmen, but the General wouldn't stop shooting.

"No! Stop!" I screamed, bolting up in bed. Sweat oozed down my face.

The light flicked on. Bjorn peered at me from his side of the room. "Are you okay Jaime?"

I looked at him dumbly. "Ye—yes. I'm okay. It's just a dream."

Ever since the incident at the marketplace, I became intrigued by the Basques. I reasoned that if I were to make my life in this country, I had better get to know its people. I began to keep a small diary in my pocket and write about my encounters with them, no matter how minute. It became an obsession with me. An escape.

I wrote alone, at night, on a pier about three kilometers downriver where I wouldn't be disturbed by the chatter of my roommates. It was both an exercise of the mind and of the body. I would tug on my jogging pants, knot the laces of my Reeboks, and canter along the river to my favorite knoll by the harbor where I could watch the city lights. In that secluded spot, I would make an entry to my diary or write to my sister and family in the best prose I could dream up. The diary became a friend, a confidant with whom I could share my deepest fears.

If I was not taking cultural lessons from Dona Moncha, I would wander around Bilbao to get familiar with my surroundings. I jogged often to keep in shape. I discovered that the Nervion River divided the city into two locales. The barrios south of the river which included Casco Viejo, Santucho, Indaucho, and the Financial District made up Bilbao proper while the barrios north of the river made up the immediate suburb: Zarzuela, Arrangoiti, Zabalburu, and Deusto, where I lived. Farther west, mimicking the flow of the Nervion sprawled the industrial towns of Santurce, Barcaldo, and Cachondo.

During these times of solitude, Bilbao couldn't have been more depressing. The city with its cluster of smokestacks was so drab it was hard to imagine a worse place to live. Everywhere I looked, I saw decrepit old foundries obscured by overcast skies which seemed to never go away. I was sure there was a sun hiding behind those jaundiced clouds but it was too disgusted with the city to grace it with its presence.

But even as I wallowed in self pity, I sensed that this town had in store for me phenomenal experiences which would affect my life forever. I sensed it in the air, living and breathing, engulfing me with its arms. There was an unsettled quality about it that was both exciting and frightening. I felt it during my walks, saw it on the faces of people I met, reminding me of the disturbing incident at the marketplace. It was like sitting on a barrel of jet fuel with someone next to you toying with a book of matches.

☼ 3 The Mystery Man

"What is this?" I asked, poking at a bowl of what looked like gross tentacles swimming in black crud. I moved the tentacles around with a toothpick.

"That's baby octopus in black ink," Iñaki said, offended. Somewhere in the bar, a jukebox blared.

"Is it edible?"

Iñaki rolled his eyes. "Of course it's edible."

Still in doubt, I offered the repulsive bowl to Cliff, the intern from London who shrank back and wrinkled his nose. Grunting in exasperation, Iñaki speared a piece of tentacle with a toothpick and shoved it in his mouth, proving to our squeamish little group that it was indeed edible. A bead of black ink dribbled from his lip, eliciting an effeminate grimace from Cliff.

The Band Of Gypsies

It had been three weeks since I arrived and I was endlessly bombarded with Spanish culture down to the gastronomical side of things. The initial shock was gone and my spirits had somewhat lifted, thanks to the letter I received from my father telling me that Marina had come home from the convent. "She's seeing a therapist and doing a little better," my father wrote. "It's going to take a little time, Jamie, but I think you may be hearing from her soon."

A peal of laughter broke into my thoughts and I glanced around the bar and saw a party in full swing: Elena at the counter joking around with Iñaki and Cliff, Bjorn gazing at her from the pinball machine, and Allison surrounded by ogling men. I now understood why Allison dated so much. She was easily the most stunning woman in the room, without exception, and that included the gorgeous Spanish coeds Iñaki brought with him to the party. She was supposed to be Elena's roommate from California, although from what I had seen, she was hardly ever home. I hadn't spoken a word to her except for the introductory *Encantado* or *Glad to meet you.*

Her beauty was hard to describe, it went beyond earthly metaphors. She had the face of a cherub, round-shaped and unblemished made classic by a pulpy heart-shaped mouth. She had the most limpid eyes I had ever seen, the bluest of tanzanites perched on white silk. And of course, there was that boyish blond hair with a little fly away at the back. At one point during the evening, she caught me watching her from afar, and I quickly averted my gaze. I didn't want her to get the wrong impression.

"Venga Elena!" someone bellowed behind me. I turned at the commotion. In the middle of the floor, Elena had broken into a sultry dance. People clapped her on. Her movements were slow, primitively erotic. Winking at the men gathered around her, she lifted her arms above her head, hips swaying with the music. I stood petrified. Coming from a repressed country like the Philippines, I had never seen this display of open sensuality. But more intriguing to me than her undulating form was the amusing discovery that she had captivated the heart of my bunkmate Bjorn; I caught him swooning at her with dreamy eyes.

Iñaki bought everyone a round of drinks, then caught my arm. "I called the company," he said in English. "You'll start in three weeks."

"Three weeks! I was supposed to start next week."

"Yes, I know. But they want someone fluent in Spanish. I couldn't take the chance of the company rejecting you. This will buy you a little time." He saw the worry in my eyes and added, "No te preoccupes, amigo. Don't worry. You'll be fine. Just practice your Spanish. Anyway, you really ought to see the city first. You know, get the feel of it, absorb the culture. That's the beauty of the exchange program."

I nodded, not mollified by his laissez-faire attitude. I was banking on my traineeship for my living allowance. If I blew it now, my stay in Spain would be finished. *Make it work*, I told myself. *You can't go back.*

Jose Mari stalked over to us, chafing like a blister. He whispered something to Iñaki, and I couldn't help but notice that something was bothering him, for his face was florid and his hands clenched into tight fists, and as I followed his gaze wondering what had triggered this animosity in a fairly easy-going man, I saw to my increasing curiosity that it was the fellow hovering over lovely Allison, a Spaniard about my age, twenty-two or twenty-three, dressed in all black, quite handsome with a dashing Zorro-esque stance. All he needed was a mask and he'd really draw in a crowd.

I fixed an eye at Allison who was too enthralled by her Latin friend to even notice Jose Mari's displeasure.

I turned to Iñaki. "Who's he?"

Iñaki curled his lips. *"Francisco,"* he said.

I stared at the mystery man. All I could think of was the Señora's earlier outburst.

☼ 4 Mountain Bandits

It was a sweaty night in Bilbao. Shirts glued to our backs like flypaper. The smell of olive oil permeated. Smoke rose off the just-emptied frying pan.

"Por Dios, I can't eat this anymore," Elena exclaimed at her smoking plate. She stuck her tongue out. "Look at this. Every day, the same old crap."

Bjorn and I looked at her numbly then shifted our gaze to the food on our plates: Spanish baguettes, fried eggs, lumpy chunks of Portuguese sardines swimming in green olive oil. My stomach rolled.

"You're right," I said, putting my fork down. "Let's eat out."

It had been seven weeks since I arrived and I had gotten some of my confidence back. Things didn't seem so bleak. Mariposa had called. I was to report to work the next day. More importantly, my sister had written me and the news was positive. "I'm back in school," she announced. "I started taking yoga classes with Mrs. Vrashni at the community center. It's helping a little. I try not to think about what happened. "

Except for Allison who seemed to be always on a date with some dashing young Spaniard, I came to know everyone. It was during this period that my friendship with Bjorn and Elena blossomed, for with Allison absent on most times and Cliff out with his English friends from work, we were naturally thrown together.

We chose a place called La Cerveceria, an open air beer garden alongside the Nervion River that served only ale and rotisserie chicken. Although we all spoke English, we conversed in Spanish.

We sat outdoors among a mish-mash of picnic tables spread out on a grassy lawn. Around us stood a grove of knuckled mulberry trees along whose branches glowed a profusion of red and green lights. Across the street flowed the Nervion River, its muddy waters pink from a dying sun. Couples promenaded along the river walk.

We gorged on three baguettes of pan, a pitcher of draft beer, and two plump chickens browned and basted in a mixture of rosemary and olive oil.

Elena dipped a piece of bread into the platter and popped it into her mouth. Closing her eyes, she chewed on it languidly. "Hmmm, muy bueno," she moaned as Bjorn and I looked on. She was easily the most provocative woman I had ever met, made even more provocative tonight by a white dress that bared her legs. There was something earthy about her; a rawness that could heat up your blood.

Taking a sip of the beer, she leaned back and stared at the

scintillating river. "Bilbao has got to be the most enchanting place I've ever been to," she said, sweeping an arm at the city and its half-finished ships. Oddly enough, Bjorn and I agreed. Bilbao, for all its imperfections, was beginning to grow on us. It was not its physical attributes that made it bewitching, but rather its radiant personality. Within it was a breadth of life palpitating like a beating heart. It could be its inherently Castilian ways: the nightly ritual of couples promenading along the river duded up in their evening bests, the subsequent visit to the bars for a glass of aperitif, the frenetic flirting that ensued, the uninhibited dancing in the streets—they all seemed a part of the everyday life in Bilbao. Even its constant obsession with politics had become fascinating.

Elena sighed. "Brazil is so different, at least the part where I come from."

"What part of Brazil did you come from, Elena?" Bjorn asked with half-closed eyes.

"Oh, it's a small town in the northeastern part of the country. I grew up on a ranch."

"A real ranch? With cows and horses?" I asked.

"Yes. My father was a big landowner."

"You're lucky to have a place like that to go back to," I said. I had nothing.

But she shook her head. "We lost the whole place...even my family."

"Oh...I'm sorry," I said.

"How did it happen?" Bjorn asked.

She shrugged. "It was a long time ago. We lived on the wild side of Brazil, you see. We had to post guards at night just to keep the robbers out. Mountains and jungles everywhere. One day, while the crew was out herding cattle, the bandits came down from the mountains and burned everything down."

"Jesus," I said.

"I was about ten. I had just finished helping my mother in the kitchen, cutting up the onions and tomatoes and making the sauce for dinner. My brother and I were playing in our secret hiding place at the back of the house. It was about five o'clock in the evening. I remember how muggy it was because my dress kept sticking to my leg.

"I heard a rumble in the distance. Lots of horses. At first I thought they were the ranch hands coming home from the round up, but there seemed too many of them." Her voice lowered. She was almost talking to herself. "Normally, I would have come out and run up to my father. But that day, I didn't. I don't know why, but I had this feeling that something terrible was about to happen. Anyway, they galloped into the yard with their guns and torches, and the shooting started. One after the other. Pop, pop, pop. Just like that.

"They shot at everyone in sight; the maids, the stable hands, the driver. I saw our gardener fall. Mario, his name was. His head was squirting all this blood on his shirt. I couldn't move. All I could do was grab my baby brother and hold him under the fallen logs where we were hiding. My aunt who took care of us from the time we were born came out calling for us, and a man rode up to her and swung this machete. It was awful. Her head flew off and all I could do was cry.

"They burned everything down, including the house. My mother was in it. Later I found out that they ambushed my father and the crew in the mountains of Santo Domingo."

Bjorn's mouth sagged open. I guess he had never heard of such violence in Sweden. I, on the other hand, understood her perfectly for in a country like the Philippines where serfdom and tribal wars still existed, it was a normal occurrence.

"So what did you do?" Bjorn asked.

"I waited for them to leave. Except of course, they didn't. They continued on their rampage all night. They even butchered my pet horse. I remember them skinning the animal and driving a stake through its body to barbecue. It was the most grotesque thing I had ever seen.

"I was afraid that my brother would cry out. But Pepito, he was good. I think he knew they were bad men, and that they would kill us if they found us. I know they would have raped me." Her voice trailed off. "...like they did the maid."

"Like they did to the what?" I asked. I didn't know if I heard her right.

"The maid. Lorena. She was a beautiful woman, and they saved her for last. They tore off her clothes right there in the yard not ten feet away from us, and raped her." She closed her eyes. "Fifteen men took turns at her all night, sometimes more than once. I was shaking in fear and crying my heart out." Elena stopped talking.

"Then what happened?" Bjorn prodded.

"They finished with her at dawn and shot her in the forehead."

"God," I said. "So what happened to you?"

She lit a Ducado, inhaled. Her hand shook. "When they rode out, I quickly grabbed my brother and ran in the opposite direction. We walked for four days in the wilderness eating only wild berries and grasshoppers. I remember being afraid because of the headhunters. They killed one of our vaqueros before."

"Headhunters?" Bjorn asked in disbelief.

"Yes, headhunters. They kill you and shrink your head for ornament. It was supposed to drive away evil spirits." She looked him in the eye. "Then they eat the rest of you."

Bjorn groaned and I almost died laughing inside had the story not been so terrifying.

"Well did you run into any of them?" Bjorn prodded, completely entangled in the web.

"Yes, on the third day. They had captured a man and lashed him to a post. I think he was a bandit because I knew they had passed that way on the way to the ranch. Anyway, I could tell from his wounds that they had kept him alive for several days while they recited chants and incantations." At this, Bjorn gave a wild shiver but Elena was not finished.

"The man was naked and his penis had been cut off. Just this pink stub, dripping blood. It's always the first thing to go. And the ears and the toes. They're like delicacies."

Bjorn looked like he was about to be sick but if Elena noticed it, she kept it to herself. "I was praying for them to kill him for what his bandit friends did to my family. So we stayed behind the bushes and watched."

"Did they?" Bjorn.

"Yes. On the same night. They finished their chants and the witch doctor stepped forward holding this long machete. Knowing what was about to take place, the man started screaming for help. My brother was so terrified that he buried his face on my chest. But I watched. The witch doctor grabbed hold of the man's hair, pulled it back to the post to expose the neck, and started sawing through it with the machete." She shut her eyes. "There were these terrible screams. And so much blood. When the head was completely cut off with all this meat hanging from the bottom, the witch doctor held it up like some kind of a trophy and started walking around with it.

"Then he raised it up like so..." At this, Elena raised her hands over her head. "...and jabbed it onto a stake." She brought her hands down with emphasis. "I'll never forget the grimace on that face."

Bjorn wiped his brows with his sleeves. "So—so what did you do?"

"We got the hell out of there. We reached town the next day and I reported what happened to the policia."

"But how were you able to live since?" I asked.

"Oh, my aunt adopted us and moved us to Rio. She was a good woman, treated us like her own. She even sent me to a good school at Sao Paolo." She stared at us. "The point is, I learned to take care of myself after that. Made me tough. It's a strange world we live in."

The sound of a backfiring engine interrupted our conversation. A black motorcycle roared by at a breakneck speed. A man was on the driver's seat with a blond woman perched precariously behind him. I looked at them in amazement. My god. It's...

"Allison," Elena confirmed. "With Francisco." Shaking her head, she gazed out with concern at the rapidly disappearing tail light.

The Band Of Gypsies

◆◆◆

"I discovered this place last week," Elena said as we strolled down the riverwalk towards our apartment. Like a scene from a Moorish fable, the Deusto Bridge towered in front of us with a quarter moon hovering over its parapet.

"Okay, careful now," Elena said as she led us down a steep flight of steps into a bar that looked more like a dungeon than a place to drink. It was no more than a dark cavern lit up by kerosene torches and on whose walls were pegged swords and shields of a medieval era. Wrought-iron chandeliers dangled from the ceiling.

The place reeked of wine which seemed to be coming from the wooden barrels stacked behind the stone counter. On a makeshift stage stood two men both of whom sported greased-back hair, black pants, and ruffled white shirts. One played a guitar and the other, a maracas.

The bartender, a bearded man with an eye patch nodded to Elena. "A ver chavala. Que te lo pongo?"

"Vino blanco para mi y rojo para mis amigos," Elena declared. She turned to us. "Isn't this great?" Bjorn and I agreed. With the costumed musicians and the titillating gitano music, it was without a doubt 'lo typico Espanol.' I drank the wine and found myself floating. My eyes latched on to Elena who had slinked over to the center of the room and began a swaying dance. She was mesmerizing to watch, her motions so fluid she seemed one with the music. Bjorn breathed heavily next to me and I knew from his wistful expression that he had become hopelessly smitten by the woman.

Elena beckoned to us. "Baila con migo, amores. Dance with me," she coaxed with a finger. Her body slithered like a snake. In a trance, I did; slowly, sensually. Her movements were contagious and I soon found myself drifting with her. I waved to Bjorn so he wouldn't feel left out, but he was either too shy or too dumbfounded to come forward.

Excusing myself from Elena, I walked up to the bar and dragged him across the room. It took a certain amount of prodding to get him to loosen up, but when he finally did, he really got into it. He did a wild version of a spas-dance; a lot of swinging arms and bobbing of the head.

When a slow tune came on, I quietly eased out of the dance floor. The bartender, noticing my obvious exit, leaned over the counter. "What's the matter, my friend. You don't like?"

"Who, Elena?" I laughed nervously. "Of course I do. Who wouldn't? But my roommate wants her even more." In reality, I didn't think I was ready for a relationship. With all that was going on in my life, it was a complication I couldn't afford. Anyway, what I really needed was a friend. Someone I could grab on to so I wouldn't fall off the cliff.

I left the bar and walked along the river to our apartment, pleased with myself for having escaped a potentially compromising situation. On one hand, I thought I really had something going with Elena, and could have pursued it if I really wanted to. But on the other hand, I knew I wasn't ready for a fling and would have surely chickened out when the time came for bedding. Worse, it would have put a strain on my friendship with Bjorn, something I wanted to avoid.

No, I thought. It's better this way. Anyway, I couldn't stay up late. *The next day was my first day of work.*

☼ 5 Aphrodite's Spell

The alarm clock rang and I stumbled out of bed, vaguely aware of Bjorn's swaddled form. I yawned sleepily, frowning at the lump. How could he breathe covered up like that?

Fighting the urge to yank the sheets, I grabbed my pants, staggered into the bathroom, and squinted at a dense vapor hovering over the shower stall. I squared my shoulders. Oh well, I thought. Another cold shower. Not the end of the world.

Clambering into the stall, I turned on the tap. The pipes shuddered violently. I held my breath, anticipating an icy blast. To my pleasant surprise, I found the water wonderfully refreshing. It jarred me awake from my dazed condition and got the torpid blood flowing in my veins. I opened my mouth...drank in the cold drops. Aahhh, Bilbao water... straight from the mountains of Vizcaya. I wondered why no one around here drank it.

After five minutes of furious scrubbing, I got out of the stall, trying to fight off a mounting panic. I told myself not to worry, that it was just like the first day of school, no different.

The analogy helped. By the time I finished shaving, I was actually looking forward to the day. I tried to remember which bus line to take. Was it the 15 Zarzuela or the 5 Caranza?

Tramping into the bedroom, I opened my mouth to awaken Bjorn and stopped dumbfounded. For a moment, I thought I had gone into the wrong room. There on the bed, white thighs and all, red toes wriggling seductively, sat Allison. She had pushed herself up in bed and wrapped a thin sheet around her body, but her shoulders were bare and a substantial amount of cleavage was showing. I tried to speak, and only managed a stutter.

Allison ran her fingers through her hair, the bedsheet falling ever so slightly to reveal more swell. "They kicked me out last night," she said in English, jerking a thumb at the partition wall.

"Who...Bjorn and Elena?"

"Yeah. When in the world did that happen?"

I shrugged. "Last night, I guess."

"Can I have a cig?" She pointed at the pack of Ducados sitting on the desk.

"Sure, help yourself. I'm trying to quit." I slipped into my shoes, double-looped the laces, then walked over to the dresser and picked out a tie. The striped one my mom gave me for my twenty-third birthday.

"Wrong tie, Jaime," Allison said. She blew smoke up the ceiling. "Try the paisley one."

"This?"

"Yep. It's more with it. Where do you work anyway?"

"At Mariposa Industria," I said. "It's my first day. You?"

"Banco de Oro at Avenida Arriaga. It's near Zarzuela."

"Hey, I work near there. Is the busline 15 Zarzuela or 5 Caranza?

"Zarzuela. The Caranza heads in another direction and will take you all the way to the next town." She stubbed out the cigarette and stood up. The sheet fell lower and she had to clutch it in front of her to hold it up. "If you wait, we can ride together," she said.

"Sure. I'll be in the kitchen." I began to walk out, but stopped. "You may want to wait a couple of minutes. The water is freezing cold."

She laughed. "Isn't this the pits? I can't remember the last time I took a hot shower."

◆◆◆

The bus stop was two blocks away at the foot of the Deusto Bridge where the Nervion River veered west towards the Bay of Biscay. It was a bright spring morning with lots of sunshine and a toasty breeze. A strong sun hovered overhead, forming a yellow dot against the periwinkle sky.

We walked down the sloping hill, two eager interns in business suits; mine, a custom tailored gabardine with pleated baggy pants, hers, a burgundy Chanel with thigh-length hem. To a passerby, we must've looked like a pair of investment bankers ready to confront the financial problems of the world. I felt exhilarated.

We entered the bridge's first tower, scampered down a

drafty stairwell, and exited underneath, finding a bus stop crowded with men in blue coveralls. There must have been thirty of them, all wearing yellow hardhats, all sporting gloomy casts on deeply lined faces. No one spoke.

"Who are these people?" I whispered.

"They're shipbuilders," Allison whispered back.

"They sure don't talk much, do they."

She sighed. "It's dangerous work, Jaime. Eight people got killed last month when their scaffolding fell into the water. They already lost ten this year and its not even May yet. See that guy over there by the kiosk?" She chinned at a man staring vacantly at the river.

I nodded.

"He lost two sons in the last accident. I heard them talking about it last week on the ride home."

My mouth fell open.

"Life is tough here, Jaime. Some of these guys are barely surviving." She brushed an errant hair from her forehead. "But watch them after work. You'll see the transformation."

We got on a red bus and found it crowded with commuters. They regarded us openly, and I'm not talking about discreet glances designed to satisfy one's curiosity, but straight-on, in-your-face stares that made you feel like you had something on your nose. Allison stood out because she was blond and beautiful, I stood out because I was brown, and well, different. On top of that, we were *extranjeros*, the word Spaniards snidely refer to foreigners.

Even in the morning when her guard was down, Allison was still intoxicatingly beautiful. Her aura radiated around the bus like a spring morning sun mesmerizing the men who couldn't help but ogle at her. I could only imagine what was going through their dirty little minds as they secretly undressed her. But such is the nature of men, I found myself doing the same.

She was not at all what I expected. Her obvious popularity with men tricked me into forming a rash judgment on her character, for up until that morning, I had envisioned her as a conceited young woman with a bad attitude who wouldn't give me a moment's notice.

On the contrary, she seemed not to care about her looks, and in fact, wore very little make up. She always had a ready smile for me, and for the other people on the bus. But what really made her attractive in my eyes was her unpretentiousness, I felt that I could talk to her without having to play games.

We made an honest attempt to talk in Spanish, not only to improve our skills of the language, but also to heighten the feeling of foreignness. And while at times we would make inadvertent lapses into English if the right Spanish word escaped us, that was largely pardonable.

The bus took us through winding roads, passing stark shipyards and factories. This was the industrial part of town from which all of the soot was originating, and as we traversed through this highly polluted area, I began to notice a sickly haze in the air that was almost green in appearance. It hung over the buildings like a veil. To the left of us was the river with its flotilla of unfinished ships, some as high as ten stories upon which blue uniformed workers braved the uneven planks of scaffoldings. Giant cranes clawed at rusty steel pipes, lifting them off the ground and dumping them onto the ships' decks.

A few more miles and the buildings became newer, more modern. Shipyards gave way to rising warehouses and office buildings.

Two blocks from my stop, Allison touched my arm. "Yours is coming up," she said.

I nodded nervously. The time of reckoning. "Where's yours?"

"Two stops after."

I agonized whether to ask her out to lunch, but decided against it. "What time do you get off?" I asked.

"Five-thirty. You?"

I looked at her pretty face and was about to say the same thing but held back. "I—I don't know just yet. It's my first day."

The bus came to a jerky stop and people filed out. I got off last.

"Well, if I don't see you on the bus, I'll see you in the apartment," she said. I didn't know if I imagined it but I thought I detected a note of disappointment in her voice. She touched my arm. "Good luck, Jaime."

I watched the bus drive off, never taking my eyes off her. We were still staring at each other from across the distance when the bus disappeared around the bend.

Sighing, I turned to face my destiny. Anxiety quickly took hold. I had never worked a single day in my life. This would be the first time I would be accountable for what I did.

Mariposa Industria was a U-shaped building four stories high, housing both its administrative offices and factory. For reasons of convenience, the former seemed to occupy the front wing of the structure, and as I stood on the sidewalk reflecting on what was to be my daytime domicile in the next seven months, I noticed that the building was quite old, perhaps vintage 1920's, and made of bricks, except the bricks were no longer red, but a sooty brown from the constant onslaught of smoke. Even the pavement was grimy, dusting my newly shined shoes with each step. Behind the administrative building occupying the rear wing was the factory that doubled as a warehouse and I could see, through an open gate, bright sparks flying off the welding machines. It was a chaotic place with lots of banging and drilling.

The entire lot was bordered by a cyclone fence, at the front of which was a gate and an outpost manned by a uniformed security guard reading a copy of El Pais. I cleared my throat.

"Is Mr. Saturnino in?" I asked in accented Spanish.

The man lowered the paper and squinted at me with guarded eyes. I repeated the question. It took three tries but he was able to get it in the end. Nodding his head, he picked up the phone and rattled a few sentences in Spanish—much too fast for me to understand.

I shrugged and began to watch a wobbly crane unload large sheets of metal from a rig, and as I watched this laborious proceeding, I couldn't help but squirm, for there were workmen directly underneath the path of the crane. "Eh," the guard said.

"Perdona me? You're talking to me?" I asked.

He said yes and pointed me to the entrance. "Tercer piso." Third floor.

He pulled out a Habanos and lit up, sucking smoke and soot into his lungs and when he saw me watching him, he extended the pack. "Fumas?" he asked.

Early on I learned that Spaniards had a habit of offering cigarettes to strangers as though they were doing them a favor, and while I was tempted to take one, I didn't know the protocol about smoking in the workplace, so I shook my head and said no thanks.

Tramping into the building, I came upon a small lobby with gaudy green paint and fluorescent lights that were blinking erratically. The elevator was to my right, a formidable unit with heavy steel door and a small square window in the middle; the type you pull out and walk into.

As I was waiting for the elevator, a handsome woman of about thirty walked into the landing from the side door, her arms loaded with folders. She scrutinized me from head to toe, as if trying to decide whether I was an intruder or a visitor, and whether or not she should talk to me.

Even though I was wearing a suit, I was arguably the only Asian she had ever seen and might have been mistaking me for a gypsy. With my thick long hair, dark eyes, and high cheekbones, I really did look like one and wouldn't have been surprised if she dashed out of the lobby and reported me to the guard.

Her curiosity must've won out because she asked, "De donde eres?" Where are you from? It quickly dawned on me that she wasn't even thinking about intruders, she just wanted to know what planet I was from.

I said, "Filipinas."

"Where is that?" she asked, possibly thinking I was pulling her leg, which I might add was wickedly sexy.

"About ten thousand miles from here," I answered. Actually, I didn't have any idea. I just wanted to impress her.

She made an 'ah' with her mouth and tried to think of the next word to say.

"I live in a tree house," I said.

She sucked in her breath. When she saw I was kidding, she burst out in laughter. "Que malo," she said. How bad you are.

"Actually, I have an appointment with Mr. Saturnino. Do you know him?"

"Ah, Mr. Saturnino. Si, si. El gran jefe. The big boss. Ven, ven," she said, motioning me to follow her.

The offices were as chaotic as the factory. There was an incessant chatter about it that was uniquely Spanish as people called out to each other from across the room, their long distance conversations peppered every now and then with colorful and sometimes sexist remarks. Oddly enough, no one seemed to be bothered by them. The workers' desks were a jumble of purchase orders, sales slips, and accounting journals, stacked so high I wondered if they would ever get to them. Everywhere I looked, I saw people pounding at adding machines as if computers hadn't been invented. In comparison to the offices in Manila, Mariposa was decades behind the times.

I followed the woman like a puppy dog with her being my only ticket to Mr. Saturnino, and whenever she encountered people she knew, she would wave at them importantly as if to say, 'Hey everyone, get a load of the extranjero I just dragged in from the street. Doesn't he look hysterical?'

We entered a well-lit corridor with small glassed-in offices lined up in a row, and stopped in front of the largest one. A woman with a big bouffant was seated at a desk outside the office pounding away on a typewriter. She looked up and smiled—a glistening slash of red across a caked-up face. "Esto es el extranjero?" she asked.

"Si," the woman leading me said. As I watched dumbly from the sidelines, they engaged in a lengthy discussion about me, making elaborate gestures to each other, modulating their voices to the tone of the dialogue. I smiled. In the short time I had been living in Bilbao, I discovered that Spaniards loved gestures, it was their way of adding color to their words. When someone wants a check at a restaurant, he normally pantomimes the shape of the bill, while at the same time verbally asking the waiter for it. Redundant as it may sound, it effectively closes the prospect of any misunderstanding that he indeed wants his check.

And so when the two ladies in front of me were absolutely sure they had understood each other and that indeed I was looking for Mr. Saturnino, the woman with the nice legs turned to me. "Mr. Saturnino's secretary will take care of you now."

I nodded. As an afterthought, I asked, "What's your name?"

"Txeli."

"Txeli," I repeated, liking the sound of it. An authentic Basque name. "Encantado a conocerte, Txeli, " I said valiantly. Enchanted to know you; one of the few gallant phrases I learned in Bilbao.

On first impression, Mr. Saturnino looked like a Spanish version of a mafioso underscored by his heavily jelled hair, double breasted suit, and two-toned tango shoes. All he needed was a hat which I suspected was somewhere in the room, and as I made a brief scan of my ornate surroundings, I thought to myself, *this is getting weirder by the minute.* Sure enough, I found the hat on a cherry wood coat rack, a conservative black fedora with a cream colored band.

"Ah, Mr. Aragon," he said grandly. "Sit down, sit down. Welcome to Mariposa."

I did, praying that I would remember my 'good' Spanish. I had been doing so well.

Saturnino studied my dossier, brows knitted in concentration, once in a while clearing his throat as if he were about to speak, and each time he did this, I would lean forward attentively only to be greeted by a soft 'Hmmm' as he riveted his eyes back to the folder. At long last, he looked up and eyed me contemplatively. I held my breath.

"Presopuesto!" he exclaimed, as if graced by a sudden enlightenment. "I'm going to put you in forecasting."

"Forecasting," I repeated.

"Yes. Financial forecasting. We're asking a bank for a loan and I need a good forecast."

Great, I thought. My first day of work and he's going to put me in forecasting. I didn't even know how to read their numbers which uses commas instead of periods and periods instead of commas. But I didn't say anything, determined to fake it to the end.

"Gabriela!" Saturnino bellowed, making me jerk up in my chair. "Bring Señor Joacquin down here to show the chaval around the place. And find Señor Aragon a cubicle, pronto."

With that, he took the cigar box from his desk and offered me a puro. Smoke a cigar in an office? But he was the boss so I extended my hand.

"Ah-ah-ah," he said, wagging a manicured finger. He

grabbed a couple of cigars from the box, snipped the ends off each one, and dipped them in the brandy decanter he had on his desk. He made sure he had soaked the ends thoroughly before handing me one. He touched a match to it.

I broke into a coughing fit. "It's a Cubano," he bragged. "They use horse shit for fertilizer. Makes it stronger." He laughed at his own joke and blew a cloud of smoke over my head. We smoked contentedly for a few minutes without uttering a word. Soon, the entire room looked like it had just been fumigated. I could barely see the guy.

That was how Señor Joacquin found us; seated on chairs, puffing up a cloud. Mr. Joacquin was as serious as Mr. Saturnino was eccentric. In fact, he looked like an undertaker with his starched white shirt and black suit. He was a bald man with a hooked nose and thin bloodless lips. His eyes were intense and heavily browed. Perhaps it was those eyes that put fear in his workers for I later noticed that whenever Mr. Joacquin was anywhere around, they'd begin to fiddle with papers.

They put me in a room bared of office accessories; there was only the desk and the overhead light. I felt I was in a police interrogation room being observed from behind secret one-way mirrors. I opened the drawers and found them empty; not a pen or a single piece of paper. Shrugging, I pulled out my diary and started to write. I didn't hear from anyone for the rest of the morning. I was dozing off on my chair when I was jolted from my stupor by the honking of horns and the wailing of many sirens. Anxious voices erupted from the hallway followed by the rattle of footsteps.

I darted out the door to see what was going on and was

horrified by what I saw.

Crowding the front gate of Mariposa was a large contingent of fire trucks and ambulances whose swirling lights filled the vicinity of the factory with eerie flashes. I could see paramedics scampering along the driveway with stretchers and gurneys two of which were completely covered by yellow tarps. I saw Mr. Saturnino down below talking to the fire chief.

"What's going on?" I asked Mr. Joacquin. People had lined up along the windows silently watching the scene.

"A sheet of metal fell off the crane," he said. "Killed some of our workers." His face looked pale and his left cheek was twitching.

"Do—do you know them?"

He nodded.

For the better part of the day, all semblance of work ceased at Mariposa as people gossiped about the accident and assigned blame to the only place they could: to Mariposa and its haphazard safety standards, and I must admit I had to agree with them, for I had witnessed those cranes myself and had in fact been dismayed to see the way the heavy sheets of metal wobbled in mid-air with all those people under it.

According to the unofficial count, seven people had been seriously wounded or killed, two of which were sliced in half by the falling blade, and even though I thought the count might have been overly exaggerated since I only saw five stretchers from the window, it didn't lessen the gravity of the situation. I noted everything down on my diary using my own reliable count. I tried not to think about the accident; my vulnerability was already at its peak. Instead, I directed my thoughts on Allison whom I would be seeing in only a few hours.

☼ 6 Adventure In Rome

I rushed out the door and charged across the street, trying to catch the 5:30 bus to Deusto. I'm late, I'm late, I thought as I spotted the red heap half a block away, winding its way along the crooked passage. I heard a screech of tires, an indignant blare of horns. Yeah, yeah, I muttered, waving at the driver of the Seat who gave me the universal finger of annoyance. I didn't know what had gotten into me; all I knew was that I had to catch that bus.

As I fell into line under a sign that said 'Parada de Autobus,' I craned my neck to see if Allison was on board. I caught a glimpse of her squinting at me from the window. She broke into a smile. "You made it," she mouthed. I gave her a wave.

Buoyant and lightheaded, I hopped into the bus. The aisle was jammed with people. But Allison had saved a seat for me at the back. "I saw you running across the street," she yelled above the din.

"Yeah, and almost got run over," I yelled back. My eyes skimmed the crowd. "Man, I can't believe this."

"Didn't I tell you? I think they're just relieved they survived another day on the scaffolding."

I nodded. I quickly realized that Allison had a unique way of viewing things; much like a psychiatrist would a patient.

"How was your day?" she asked.

The bus had slowed at the approaching stop. A huddle of workers milled under the autobus sign. I gazed at their swarthy forms, their tired weather-beaten faces, and suddenly felt depressed. "There was an accident at the office today," I said.

Allison gasped. "Wh—what happened?"

"A sheet of metal fell off the crane and killed some people." I shook my head. It had affected me more than I thought. As I gave Allison an account of the incident, I detected a certain sadness in her eyes, as though she was aware of the problems facing these people. "...and they carried five of them off in stretchers and loaded them in ambulances," I said, finishing the story.

Allison touched my arm. "I'm sorry Jaime. Your first day, too."

I nodded. We had now circled the north end of the river bank and the city skyline came into view. Bilbao, I sighed. What other gory surprises do you have in store for us?

I had planned to ask her out to dinner, even cooked up devious schemes with which to make my move. But in the end, I never worked up the nerve to do it. Why would a beautiful woman like her bother with the likes of me? She had that guy, what's his name...Francisco. And all those other men swooning over her from the university.

When we reached our Deusto apartment, another batch of interns had just arrived. Miguel, the Venezuelan from whom we hadn't heard in weeks, was among the new arrivals. Gifted with dark lashes and a perfectly chiseled face, he was handsome to the point of being unmanly. The story had it that the cad had decided to gallivant around the baroque taverns of Rome without telling anyone of his whereabouts prompting Iñaki to call his parents in Caracas, only to discover that they didn't know where he was either. But things had a way of mending themselves in Bilbao and before I knew it, Iñaki and Miguel were jesting around like long lost friends.

On a number of occasions, Allison tried to catch my eye, but I kept getting sidetracked as I wove my way towards her, first by Elena who asked me about my first day, and afterwards by Bjorn who wanted me to recount the story about the accident.

"Finally," Allison said, after I had extricated myself.

I rolled my eyes and smiled. Discreetly, I glanced around the room. No one was looking. My mouth turned dry. Ask her now, a voice inside me said. You'll never get another chance. And before I could stop myself, I heard myself say, "Allison—wo—would you like to go out to dinner with me?"

She opened her mouth to speak, but the door suddenly swung open. There at the opening stood Francisco: handsome, imposing, dressed in a black coat. He scanned the room briefly, spotted Allison, and promptly walked over to her.

"Sorry I'm late," he said, completely unaware of me. "Ready to go?"

Allison blushed. She began to turn towards me, but Francisco took her hand. "Vamonos querida. Our reservation is at eight." Before she could utter another word, he put his arm around her, whisking her away.

I stood there like a fool. Heat surged up my face. You dummy. How could you even think she'd go out with you?

I wanted to run away, hide under the bed. But as I glanced around the room feeling as puny as a bug, I realized no one had witnessed the fiasco. Well, almost no one. Iñaki and Jose Mari were standing in the middle of the room scowling after the disappearing couple. This inevitably fanned my interest. What the hell is going on here, I thought. What's up with that guy?

Filing the questions away, I joined the Venezuelan in the kitchen who was recounting his Italian horror story to Cliff, his soon-to-be roommate. Bjorn and Elena had padded over.

"I'm lucky to be alive," Miguel proclaimed about his mysterious delay. "I would have been dead by now."

"What happened?" Cliff asked wide-eyed. There was something about the way he looked at Miguel that sparked my curiosity.

"Well, the day before my flight to Bilbao, I met this girl in Rome."

"It figures," Elena said.

"But she was a beautiful girl, senorita, with a face of an angel." He brought his fingers to his lips and kissed it with flourish. "Anyway, we went out drinking all afternoon and got along very well. We sort of lost track of time. Before we knew it, it was dark."

"So your man-thing forced you to make a move," Simone, the French girl from next door scoffed.

"No, not yet, senorita. You see, I had checked out of the hostel earlier in the day because I was trying to save money. After all, I am but a poor student from Caracas. I thought I would just walk around Rome until my flight in the morning and if I got tired, I would sleep in the terminal. Makes sense, no? But, la signorina, she invited me to her house, you know what I mean?"

"Oooh boy," I said.

"Si, amigo. Oh boy is the right word. For me, it was two birds with one stone. I was going to have my room and I was going to have my girl."

"Well, did you go?"

He looked at me as though I were crazy. "Of course. You think I will pass up an opportunity like that? Anyway, she took me to her house in the suburbs of Rome. Only it wasn't an apartment like I expected. It was a big villa with swimming pool and tall fences. I saw it from the outside."

"What do you mean from the outside?" Cliff asked. He inched closer.

"You see, she made me duck under the dashboard when we drove in."

"That is a little strange, no?" Simone said.

"I felt the same way, senorita, but she said she was afraid of her mother."

Elena snickered. "So you're sneaking in? How old is this girl anyway?"

"Thirty-five."

"Thirty-five!" Everyone exclaimed in unison. "And she's still sneaking in?"

"Well, listen to the story. She drove into the garage and we walked upstairs to the house."

He paused for effect. "Guess who I found inside?"

"Her mother," Cliff said.

"No-no-no, my friend. Her son."

"Her son!" Again in unison.

"Yes, she had a son. Four years old. About just so." At this, he raised his palm in level with his hips. "But she told me it was her sister's, that she was just taking care of him. So she took the boy upstairs and tucked him in bed. Then she came down for me."

"Well?" Elena prodded.

"She took me to her bedroom."

"Come on, Miguel. Speed it up. The suspense is killing me," I said.

"She undressed me. And I her." At that, Miguel traced a CocaCola bottle with his hands to the annoyance of Simone and Elena. Seeing their irritation, he said, "I won't get into the details of this but it was wonderful. We did everything. In fact it was so good we did it again."

"Again?" The girls exclaimed in astonishment. "After how many minutes?" Simone asked.

"Five."

"Five! But how..." Elena's voice trailed off. She looked at Bjorn who shrugged.

"Anyway, senorita, as we were doing it, a car drove in. I noticed it only because she had bolted up in bed. Her face had turned white. I saw the lights on the curtains and said, 'What's the matter, querida, is it your mother?' And she said, no, it's my husband."

"Oh no," Bjorn said.

"Oh yes. She told me to dress quickly. She was so frightened she kept calling out the names of all the saints. Even ones I didn't know. She told me to hide under the bed. I said, why don't I just slip out of the window? But she became terrified. She said no, I can't. There are guards outside. As it turned out, her husband is a big time Mafioso in Rome."

"Ay, por Dios," Elena lamented.

"As you can imagine, I panicked. I hid under the bed just as her husband walked in. I was shaking. I thought, Dios, if you save me this one time, I will join the priesthood and never have another woman again." He shuddered at the memory. "But the husband, he was agitated, you know. Horny. So it was not surprising that he didn't see me. He wanted to make love, and the poor senorita was trying to avoid him. But you know how Italian men are."

"Yeah, we know how Italian men are," Elena said, winking at Simone. Both of them burst out laughing.

"Anyway, he got his way. Of course, being under the bed, I didn't know what they were doing. But five minutes later, the Mafioso guy said, Sophia, my love, you taste different tonight."

Everyone looked at each other in disgust. Cliff snickered.

"Did he find out?" Bjorn asked, once again hooked on the story.

"At this point, I didn't know because the bed was suddenly bouncing. Up, down, up down, it went. Sometimes it came so low the springs would touch my nose. And guess what he said next?"

"What?" We all leaned over.

"He said, Sophia, why are you so slippery? I think at this point, he was becoming suspicious. But Sophia was good and was faking her orgasm to get his mind off things. Anyhow, it went on like that for five minutes and then it stopped. And then I heard him say, 'you had another man tonight, Sophia.' That was when I really became afraid. The box springs creaked and I heard Sophia pleading. I heard a slap, and then another. I began to shake. Then the husband said: *If you don't come out from under the bed, payaso, I am going to shoot it full of holes.* At first I didn't know if he was talking to me until he started counting."

"Did you come out?" Bjorn asked.

"Of course. You think I wanted to die? I scrambled out of bed and I almost had an accident in my pants. This man with a mustache, he stuck a gun under my chin. Then he cocked it. Por Dios, I thought he was going to pull the trigger. But instead, he swung that thing and hit me on the side of the head, pulling the trigger at the same time." Everyone grimaced.

"It hit me right here." He pointed at the bony part behind his right ear and showed us the stitches. They were still fresh and ran from his scalp down to his left earlobe.

Everyone fell silent.

"The worst part was, I thought I'd been shot. It was so loud. I danced around the room on one leg thinking I was dying. But he only did it to scare me. The shot sent his men running and he told them to take me somewhere and get rid of me." He wiped his brows with his sleeves.

"But how did you escape?" Bjorn asked.

"Well, fortunately, the policia came. It appears that the man was already under investigation and was being staked out. When the policia heard the shot, they thought it was one of their own so they came charging in." He gave a wild shiver. "And that's how come I was late."

◆◆◆

That night, the entire group went out drinking. I decided to stay home with the excuse of having a lot of letter writing to do. Not that I was martyring myself. It's just that I had set my sights on taking out Allison anything less would have been a let-down.

After suffering through another round of self-chastening, I busied myself with my diary. I wrote a lengthy letter to Marina, sharing with her my first day at work including the thrilling bus ride with Allison. I skipped any mention of the afternoon's disaster and concentrated on the good things. She had enough things to worry about.

On the face of the envelope, I left out my name and return address. I wouldn't put it past General Sanchez to send someone up here to do me in. He had done worst things.

I had just folded the letter when I heard a tap on the door.

"Si?" I said, thinking of the Señora.

"Ja—Jaime? It's me, Allison."

Allison. My heart skipped a beat. Pushing the letter under the pillow, I padded to the door. She was standing in the hallway bathed in yellow light. Her eyes were round and big, and I noticed a little red as though she had been crying.

"Are you okay?" I asked.

She blushed. "Yes...I'm fine."

I stepped aside. "How was dinner?"

"We didn't go," she said in a hollow voice.

"You didn't? How come?"

"I was tired. I asked him to take me home."

"I'm sorry."

"Don't be. I just wanted to rest, that's all."

"I have some peaches in the fridge. Want some?"

She nodded.

I went out to get a couple. When I came back, she was sitting on the bed. "Can I just sit here for a while?"

"Yeah, sure. Mi habitacion es su habitacion. My room is your room."

She laughed at the joke.

I gave her the peach and sat down next to her. Through the open window, we could see the bridge and the stars and the moon which looked like a sliver of orange peel.

Allison bit into the fruit and wiped her lips with a napkin. Questions rose in my mind. Why did she come back? Why had her romantic date ended so soon?

"I'm sorry about tonight," she said. "Me and Francisco..."

I waved it off. "Don't worry about it. Really." Heat rose up my face.

She sighed. "You're a sensitive man, Jaime." A pause. "You remind me of someone."

"Yeah?...who?"

She shrugged. "You're so different from anyone I know. Even Francisco."

"In what way?"

"Oh, just little things. Most people take what they want. You think about it first."

"Is that good or bad?"

"Both, I guess. Good because you are sensitive to other

people's feelings, bad because you may never get what you want."

I glanced at her, unsure as to what she meant. She was staring at the moon. "This is the first day we ever really talked, did you realize that?" she said.

I nodded.

"I guess I've just been too..." She shook her head, not finishing the sentence. "Anyway, I was talking to Elena. You guys have become good friends?"

I nodded.

She was silent for a moment. The bed creaked as she leaned against the headboard. "Will you be my friend too?"

I felt a tug. "If you want."

She smiled, then stared at the moon again. "I'd like that."

☼7 The Legend Of El Lobo

I came home early from work and found Doña Moncha bent over the kitchen sink. She had a sponge in her hand. "Ah, my favorite boarder," she said. "How are you chiquito?"

"I'm fine Señora."

"And how is work. Bien?"

"Si Señora. There was a demonstration again at the plaza. I watched it from the sidelines."

"Por Dios, Jaime. You shouldn't go near those demonstrations. Muy peligroso. They are very dangerous."

"I saw that guy Allison is going out with—the one from the university. He was in the crowd with a couple of guys."

She frowned. "Who? Francisco?"

"Yes."

She opened her mouth to speak but seemed to think better of it.

"Señora, why do the Basques have so much hatred? They

seem such nice people when you talk to them."

The Señora studied me for a moment, then motioned me over to a chair. "Mira," she said, tracing a finger along the battered surface of the table. "Aqui esta España. Y dentro por el norte esta el Pais Vasco."

With a stubby finger, she proceeded to draw a map of Spain, pointing out the seven Basque provinces in the Pyrenees. It surprised me to learn that three of them were in France. "The Spanish Basques are a fierce people, Jaime. Very proud. They want full independence from Madrid." She pronounced Madrid with a Spanish lisp so that it sounded like Madrith.

"And you know the reason why?" she queried.

I shook my head.

"Because Bilbao and Barcelona are the heart of Spanish commerce. This is where the money is. Look around you, hijo. Everywhere you turn, you see banks and industry. This is the banking capital of Spain."

I nodded. The observation didn't escape me: the abundance of banks, the bustling commerce. The trait that made Bilbao ugly was the same thing making it flourish.

"The mountains of Vizcaya are rich in natural resources, Jaime. Gold, silver, copper—they all come from the Vascongadas. That is why you see a lot of factories. People from all over Spain flock over here to find work. And you know what? More than half the people in Bilbao are not Basques. They are immigrants from destitute places like Extremedura and Andalusia. I myself came from Galicia."

"But that's normal everywhere."

Doña Moncha shook her head. "The Basques are a proud

and productive people, Jaime. More so than the rest of the country. They see Madrid as a leech that will fill its coffers and squander their money on other provinces.

"Here in the Vascongadas, they never take siestas in the factories. They are always working, morning, noon, and night. Not like in Madrid where everything shuts down in the afternoon." She wagged a finger to make a point. "Not very productive."

"So money is really the issue," I said, rather disappointedly. I had given the Basque more credit than that.

"Partly, yes. But it goes much deeper than that, Jaime. It is also about history. The Basques are a different race. Remember what they were chanting during that demonstration at the marketplace? That's Euzkerra, the Basque language. No one knows where it came from."

She stood up. "Come, come," she beckoned, shuffling over to the window that overlooked the apartment buildings at the courtyard. She pointed at a brick structure across the way. "See that man sitting on the terrace?"

I followed her gaze. Through the banners of fluttering laundry, I spotted a shirtless man in boxer shorts staring blankly at the river. "Yes."

"Well, he wasn't like that before. He used to be the political leader of the terrorist group ETA. The Guardia Civil called him El Lobo or The Wolf. They had been after him for years but he always managed to stay one step ahead of them. Back then, few people knew his face so he was able to mingle with the crowd."

I squinted at the man and his underwear. He didn't look like much. "Did you know about him then? I mean as El

Lobo?"

She shook her head. "I had seen him around the marketplace and even talked to him a few times, but no, I didn't know about him. His identity was a closely guarded secret, you see, known only to a few trusted comrades. In any event, one day, a former comrade betrayed him and revealed his true identity to the police. The police came to his apartment but he was still able to evade capture.

"Frustrated and under pressure from Madrid, General Bustamante, the commandant of Bilbao's Guardia Civil, ordered El Lobo's family detained. They arrested his lovely wife Anita and his twin daughters Lily and Pilar who were freshmen at the university. They threw them in jail in Burgos and charged them with treason. It was a false charge of course but the General was using them as a bargaining peseta.

"He gave El Lobo an ultimatum: surrender peacefully or his family will be summarily executed for the terrorist acts they committed. El Lobo knew his priorities; family first before political beliefs. So he agreed to surrender."

The Señora nodded proudly towards the man. "Through a courier, he sent a message to the General. 'Sundown,' El Lobo wrote. 'At the main street of Guernica.' He knew he was sacrificing himself, that he might not come out of it alive. But he didn't care. All he wanted was his family's safety. Of course, the General had other ideas in mind."

My stomach churned and the Señora continued, "True to his word, El Lobo came at the prearranged time. Alone. He didn't want any complication that would endanger his family.

"El Lobo faced the General on the other end of the street. Rifles were pointed at him. 'Okay General, I am coming in,' El

Lobo called out from his end of the street. 'But release them first.' The General nodded to his men and one of them opened a van and let out El Lobo's family. Rumor had it that they were a haggard lot. Their eyes were sunken and their cheeks like so." The Señora sucked in her cheeks, but didn't get the desired effect.

"Seeing their pitiful condition, El Lobo couldn't help but weep. Hand in hand, the women scurried down the street, fearful of the guns pointed at them. What happened next no one really knows for sure. There were so many versions of it. The official one was that El Lobo pulled out a gun which started all the shooting." The Señora shook her head. "It really doesn't matter at this point whether it's true or not. The only thing that matters is that the three women ended up dead. Rumor had it that they shot the twins so many times they were almost cut in half."

I groaned, and the Señora nodded. "El Lobo was so traumatized at seeing his wife and children killed all he could do was weep. He never recovered after that. He became insane and they incarcerated him in an asylum in Burgos." The Señora sighed. "Then they operated on him."

"Operated on him? Why, was he sick?"

"No, but rumor had it that they wanted to turn him into a vegetable. It is a game of will, you see. The General wanted to humiliate the Basques and use El Lobo as an example. So they gave him a lobotomy and sent him back home for everyone to see. It is a bigger blow to ETA than simply killing him."

She put her hand on mine. "So you see how bad it is? El Lobo is only one example of Madrid's many atrocities."

As I walked along the river that night, I couldn't help but feel that our peaceful little group might have inadvertently blundered into the early stages of an uprising. I thought about Beirut, how a simple gunbattle in the streets had ignited into a civil war and thought, God help us.

◆◆◆

There had been a small development in our group. It had something to do with Miguel and Cliff. From the moment Miguel arrived in Bilbao, the two had become an inseparable pair. They went out in all hours of the night and spent an inordinate amount of time locked up in the bedroom. It got so that Bjorn and I often broke into knowing smiles whenever they were in one of their closed-door sessions. Not that we were being catty, we just thought it funny at the time.

One morning, I woke up early to go jogging along the river and caught Cliff giving Miguel a shoulder massage in the kitchen. They broke away when they saw me, but not before I caught a glimpse of the rosiness on Cliff's face.

I pretended not to notice. "Buenos dias," I said brightly.

"Hey, amigo," Miguel said from his chair. He seemed more comfortable about the arrangement than Cliff who had shuffled over to the coffee pot.

"So how is work, Jaime?" Miguel asked.

"Great," I said. "I'm finally getting into the swing of things."

"That is good, my friend. Listen, why don't you have lunch with us sometime? Bjorn and I work in the same company."

"At that engineering firm?"

"Yes. It is in downtown Bilbao. It will be fun, yes?" He

winked at me. "I will even introduce you to some of the señoritas at the office."

"Fine. Just let me know when." I glanced at him on the way out. His debauched adventure in Rome and clandestine affair with Cliff simply didn't jibe. I wondered if he was bi.

Miguel's arrival brought the number of interns living in the Señora's building to thirteen. As one might imagine, our nights became hectic.

There was a bar in town we had picked as our hang out. It served the cheapest wine and tapas in town. It was called El Caracol, a brick-roofed stucco dive with a four-stool counter, a jukebox, a pinball machine, and a pair of battered tables on the patio overlooking Plaza San Pedro. It was not unusual for the thirteen of us to spend the evening in that bar, talking about work, getting to know the newcomers, making plans for the summer. Peanuts and sweet sherry accompanied these fetes.

As for Allison and I, we became kindred spirits, drawn to each other by a force we had yet to put a finger on. It showed in the way we talked, in the way we acted, this constant awareness of each other. She could be at one end of the room talking to the other interns and I at the other and we could communicate by simply looking at each other, and whenever we got into one of these mental dialogues, we would break into amused smiles.

But it never went beyond that. Maybe we were both holding back even if for entirely different reasons. Mine was borne out of insecurity not only for my uncertain future, but also for the way in which I looked at myself as a person. To a certain extent, I still felt intimidated by her. She was so beautiful—so unattainable.

Be that as it may, there had been an evident change in Allison worth mentioning. In the last few days since our bus ride, she seemed to be spending more time with our group and less with her friends at the university. And even though I knew the possibility of it was remote, I dared fantasize that I might have been part of the reason. That is not to say she had stopped seeing Francisco. On the contrary, they still went out most nights.

I thought about the man. What was it about him that attracted her? Was it his physical attributes which the other female interns in the building described as dashing and sexy or something much deeper. More importantly, what was it about him that outraged Jose Mari, Inaki, and of all people, the Señora? I found it strange how red faces surfaced whenever he happened to be around.

One evening on my way home from the docks, I spotted Francisco with the same two men he was with at the demonstration at Plaza Vasco. They were scurrying towards the dormitories, lugging on their backs what looked like a couple of bulky gym bags. As they went through the doors, one of them broke rank and made his way into the shadows of the trees. The man, long-haired and stocky, just stood there with the glowing tip of a cigarette. A look out? I had thought then. But what for? I wanted to raise my suspicions to Allison but was afraid of sounding too much like a jealous suitor.

☼ 8 The Premonition

"There it is!" Allison said, pointing at the red bus weaving along the riverbank. We darted into the bridge's tower, scurried down the stairs, and came out at the bus stop below.

The bus was half full. We chose a seat in front where we could have a better view of the river.

"Where do you eat lunch?" Allison asked, putting her bus pass back in her totebag.

"At the factory. I buy a ham bocadillo and eat it up on the roof with some friends. Sometimes I take a walk along the river and write."

"What do you write about?"

"Oh...letters...thoughts for my diary. You, me, my experiences here." It was as close as I ever got towards revealing my true feelings for her.

"Eat lunch with me today," she said.

I glanced at her in her navy blue jacket, white blouse, and

khakis. "Why? What's the occasion?"

"Nothing. I—I mean—if you have other plans I—."

"Don't be silly. I don't. And I'd love to." We passed the Cerveceria, its ample lawn empty of people. "But where do you want to go?"

"I thought we can check out the Jardines Bertendon."

"Cool," I said.

We agreed to meet halfway between her office and mine which was a six-block walk in either direction after which, we would proceed to the park.

I couldn't focus on work, the anticipation of a private rendezvous with Allison keeping me on edge. It wasn't a good day to be slouching off either. Señor Joacquin wanted a revised forecast for his next day's meeting with the bankers.

All morning long, I contrived all sorts of scenarios with which to make my move, from drawing her a homemade card that said 'thanks for being a friend' to buying her a red rose, eventually discarding every one of them as either too corny or melodramatic. The clock ticked at an excruciating pace.

When one o'clock finally arrived, I was so eager to leave the building that I rushed out of the door without taking my jacket. Fortunately, it was a warm day.

I found her seated at the docks with her legs dangling above the water watching a ferry boat come in. A seagull flew by and landed on the railing. A smokestack belched nearby.

"Hi there," she greeted. Getting to her feet, she gave me a hug. She regarded me appreciatively. "Look at you. You look so handsome in that denim shirt."

A warm feeling spread all over me.

"Shall we?" she said, taking my arm.

I nodded, still high from the compliment.

We strolled for a couple of blocks, cut through an alley lined with shops and cafes, took a shortcut through a tented marketplace, and came out on the other side. The Bertendon Gardens sat across the street.

I squinted at the apparition. A topiary park in the midst of the industrial center, it was a stark departure from the drabness of the neighborhood. Its carefully manicured lawn adorned with sculptured trees and bushes was like a meadow in a harsh desert. Flower beds abounded: yellow marigolds, red begonias, purple impatiens—they dazzled our eyes as we treaded our way along the graveled path towards what looked like a green pond with floating waterlilies. She picked out a sunny bench facing a pond and took out a paperbag of food from her totebag.

"I thought we were simply going to buy bocadillos from the bar across the street."

"This is better. I prepared it last night."

Curious, I opened the paperbag and found two sandwiches, two red peaches, two cups of apple yogurt, two plastic glasses, and a bottle of red wine.

"You prepared these last night?" I asked, unwrapping the sandwiches. So that's why she used that large tote bag this morning. She saw my expression and said, "Yes, Jaime, I planned it. Is that so wrong?"

"Nope," I said impishly. "In fact, it's wonderful."

A blue butterfly flew by and fluttered over a sunflower.

Allison took a deep breath and gazed at the outlying skyline. "I never thought I'd get to love this place. It's so exhilirating."

"I know."

"San Francisco seems so far away." She took on a dreamy look. "My father used to be in the army, did I tell you that? A career officer."

I shook my head, bit into the sandwich. Linguisa with sliced tomatoes.

"Well he was. He volunteered for Vietnam when I was eight. He went back twice." She smiled at the memory. "Such an adorable foolish man. You know how you look at adults as being really old at that age?"

I nodded. I had felt the same way about my dad. I thought he was old at thirty-one.

"Well, my dad was different," she said. "I had always looked at him as a handsome young man. When he came back after that first tour, he had medals all over his chest. He was like a hero, you know. Young, dashing, full of life. You know how old he was when I was born? Sixteen."

"That <u>is</u> young."

"I know. My mom was only fifteen then. They were high school sweethearts. They almost didn't get married because my dad's family didn't approve of her."

"Why?"

"She had a reputation." She tossed a pebble into the pond.

"How did you know that?"

"She told me. We're like sisters. She'd always been bitter about his family for not accepting her."

"Was she, though? Loose, I mean?"

"Depends on how you look at it. If falling romantically in love is loose, then yes. She started going out when she was twelve, sometimes with men eight years older."

"Eight years? But that would make them twenty," I protested.

She gave me a look that said, 'you're the last person I expected to say that', but all she said was, "Yes. But she never had sex with them. She was a romantic. She saw men as gallant knights on white horses ready to sweep her away."

"Is that how you see them too?"

"To a certain extent, yes. I took after her in that regard although I see fewer men fitting that knight-on-the-white horse description these days."

"I'm sorry," I said.

"Don't be. I could still find mine."

I looked at her and she blushed. She threw another pebble into the pond. "I lost my dad when I was thirteen."

"How?"

"Vietnam. Just when Saigon was about to fall. He had a child by a Vietnamese woman. Her name is Tutui. You know, like two-three with a lisp." She smiled. "Anyway, they were evacuating the city with Blackhawk helicopters and my dad was trying to get Tutui and her mom to the embassy. A maid was helping them evacuate at the time. A mortar exploded in front of them and killed them instantly. Except for the maid and Tutui who had just turned the corner and were saved by the concrete wall. She was only six."

"How terrible. Did your mom ever find out about the mistress?"

"Yes, but much later. Even my dad didn't know about Tutui until his second tour. That was when he wrote my mom. And for whatever reason, my mom understood. She said strange things happen to a person in a foreign country. She thinks it's the isolation. Everything is new and strange and a person needs something to hold on to."

I nodded. That was exactly how I felt.

"Did you ever meet Tutui?"

"Yes. My mom adopted her and brought her over. She grew up with me. She's my best friend aside from being my half-sister."

"That's a wonderful story, Allison," I said, genuinely touched.

"You see Jaime, I believe that each person has his own unique world. I have my world and you have yours. My friends—my experiences—are part of my world." She was silent for a moment. "And you are a big part of it." She caught herself. "I—I didn't mean for it to sound that way—I mean..."

"Shhh, Allison, it didn't. And I agree with you."

She smiled, happy that I understood.

"Do you agree with your mom that foreigners do strange things in foreign countries?"

She nodded. "Yes, because when you get right down to it, only our present life really matters. My life in San Francisco is nothing but a vague memory. I can't see it, I can't touch it."

She swept an arm across the park. "This is my reality now, even for only six months. This big, ugly, intoxicating city." She gave me a lopsided smile. "And you are my reality too, Jaime. And Elena. And Francisco." At the mention of Francisco, I felt a sting of jealousy but I quickly covered it up.

"Ever wonder what brought us here together?" she asked.

Man, she sure is in a psychologizing mood today. But I only said, "You mean us, as in our group?"

"No, you and me personally."

I shrugged. "Fate?"

She raised a skeptical eyebrow. "Yeeaah, but I think it's more than that."

"What?" I was getting excited.

"I don't know. Maybe we were brought here for a reason. I feel that this is only the beginning."

She gazed at the sky as if imagining some faraway place. I wished I could see what she was seeing. "There is something out there, Jaime, waiting for us, ready to affect us in a big way. Just you and me. Maybe Elena too." She shivered. "Sometimes that feeling is so intense I feel frightened by it."

Touched, I took her hand, kissed it. She blushed but didn't take her hand back. And for a brief moment, I thought I saw something akin to fear in her eyes. A wide-eyed cornered look. But she quickly covered it up.

On the way back to work, we stopped at a boutique where I tried on a white cotton shirt with a cropped collar. I badly needed one since I brought only a couple of casual shirts with me. "That looks great on you, Jaime," Allison said. "Are you going to buy it?"

I stared at the shirt. Two thousand pesetas. Twenty dollars. I was about to say yes but remembered my shaky future. I forced a smile. "Nah, I need it like I need a hole in the head."

She looked at me strangely but didn't say anything.

That lunch hour was the beginning of the most wonderful and haunting experience of my life. It affected us differently. While it irrevocably stoked my affection for her, it seemed to have had the opposite effect on her. She became distant and never repeated the invitation for lunch. It was as if she were afraid to be alone with me. I had asked her out twice, but her responses had been "Oh, I'm sorry Jaime. It's a little hectic at work" or "I already made plans." I felt spurned, unwanted, and I didn't know the reason why. It had been going so well. Rebuffed, I withdrew into a shell and built a wall around me.

She saw a lot more of Francisco; almost every night. Her days became divided between me and him. I had her company during the day and he had her company during the night. But mine lasted only for the duration of the bus ride. Whatever they did on their trysts, I didn't care to know. I would be lying if I said I wasn't jealous, because I was. Painfully so. I saw them often in the student bars of Deusto, drinking with friends at the university. During these times, Francisco would have his arm around her possessively, as if they already had a commitment to each other. Maybe that was the reason I pulled back, became reserved, which was not really in my nature.

I made it a point to avoid them. Knowing Allison, she might ask me to join them which could turn out to be really awkward.

She must have noticed this change in me because she brought it up one morning. We were standing at the foot of the bridge waiting for the bus when she asked, "Is something the matter?"

I looked at her innocently. "No, why?"

"It's just that you've been so quiet these days."

"Oh, maybe it's because I haven't received any letter from my folks." It was true about the letters but not about my detachment. In truth, I was afraid of falling in love with her. She seemed so complex; strong and at the same time weak, deep at the same time shallow—she vacillated a lot, swinging like a pendulum between me and Francisco. I didn't want to get hurt.

If I was not having success in my personal life, I was having successes at work. Mr. Joacquin became my mentor and gave me the wisdom of his experience. He insisted that financial analysis and all the concepts we learned in business school could only take me so far, that I would have to rely on my business instincts to succeed. It was hard to swallow at first. After all, it took me six years to get my degree which had given my parents a lot of grief. But I also saw the logic of it. So I listened, and learned.

One day as I was poring over our annual reports, I discovered that Mariposa had its hands on just about everything having to do with the aircraft business. It manufactured valves and spare parts for the big aircraft companies in Europe and even processed lubricants. It was in the lubricant business that I began to see something faulty. From what I could gather, Mariposa imported raw materials from Indonesia, Borneo, and the Philippines. This raw material came from a tropical plant called Nipa of which cloth, soap, and detergent were made.

A by-product of this plant was a greasy substance called Lanol from which can be processed the aircraft lubricant called Lubricus, a patented Mariposa product. But the fault rested not in the science but in the way Mariposa sourced the raw material, for they shipped it in large metal bins all the way from Asia, then processed them in Bilbao, only to ship them back to their major customers in Japan, Korea, and the Far East as the aircraft lubricant called Lubricus.

A few tons of the Lubricus also found their way into

distribution centers in Europe. I thought, how ridiculous. Why not process the Lanol in the Far East where labor was cheaper and freight to Japan, less expensive?

One morning, I broached this discovery to Mr. Joacquin and his eyes bugged out. He quickly took me to Mr. Saturnino's office and sat me down on a chair. "Tell Mr. Saturnino what you told me," Mr. Joacquin said.

So I explained my theory about processing the Lanol where it came from, in Asia, to save on labor and freight, and Mr. Saturnino nodded as if a lightbulb just blinked in his head. "You may have something there, chaval," he said, puffing on a Cubano. "In fact, it's a damned good idea. Let me bring it to the board."

As it turned out, the board approved the concept and I was given an additional three month's salary for my efforts. The next day, they took me out of forecasting and placed me in strategic planning, still under Mr. Joacquin's guidance. When I told the news to my roommates, Allison kissed me on the cheek and said, "I'm so proud of you, Jaime." For the first time in days, I felt genuinely happy.

Txeli, the thirty-something woman I met on my first day of work, became a good friend. She told me all sorts of workplace gossips. One that particularly grabbed my interest was about Mr. Joacquin and Mr. Saturnino. Of course, the bosses' dirty laundry was always the juiciest by virtue of their position in the company.

From what I could gather, it seemed that Mr. Joacquin was married to Mr. Saturnino's distant niece who worked as an analyst in the marketing department. Saturnino and Joacquin were about the same age, in their late forties. The niece, whom I had seen as a beautiful young woman, was about thirty, perhaps much too young for the middle-aged Joacquin. In any event, it now appeared that Mr. Saturnino, who himself was married to Mr. Joacquin's third cousin was having an affair with Mr. Joacquin's wife, his distant niece.

It took me a minute to connect the relationships and I had to draw a flow chart with elaborate boxes and arrows just to get it right. When Txeli was sure I understood the connections, she continued with her story. Saturnino's wife, it appeared, found out about the affair and began having one of her own with Joacquin. At first, it was just to get even with Saturnino but they ended up falling in love.

I frowned at the story. "Why don't they just swap wives?"

She laughed. "That's what everybody says."

What a soap opera, I thought. I would never have believed the story had I not known the source to be quite reliable. It came from the Saturnino family's own private chauffeur whom Txeli was dating clandestinely. I say clandestinely because the chauffeur was also married and had eight kids. It was this type of interaction that made my job so gratifying. From then on, I made it a point to seek out Txeli during our coffee breaks to get my daily dose of gossip.

☼9 The Gypsy King

The days flew by. April became May, and the weather turned balmy. Verbenas replaced the daffodils, red poppies sprouted. We were stretched out at the banks of the Nervion River, Elena, Allison, Bjorn, and a French intern named Simone when a sizable flock of river ducks floated by. There was a good mass of them, at least four thousand strong packed along the brown river with their shiny green coats. I had never seen river ducks before, let alone this many. I thought they only lived around lakes.

There was a story behind them. It seems that Bilbao is the breeding ground for these river ducks who migrate there from Andalusia during the spring and hatch their eggs along the banks of the Vizcayan Mountains where the Nervion River originates. The ducklings dwell in these mountains for a few weeks until they are strong enough to brave the rapids, after which time, they will embark on the hazardous trip down the falls, following the downstream flow of the river through Bilbao, Baracaldo, and Santurce, passing the smaller towns along the way until they reach the Bay of Biscay where they will begin their journey south to Cadiz and the Rock of Gibraltar. Simply put, they were merely hitching a ride on the river.

I remembered it as being a Sunday; we had nothing else planned so we decided to laze around the jetty and soak in the sun. We brought along a picnic basket filled with sumptuous cheeses and drippy comestibles and a couple of bottles of vintage wine. We spread blankets along the concrete platform. While it wasn't exactly a tropical paradise, it was as close as we could get to a beach in downtown Bilbao.

It was five o'clock in the evening, and we could see old Bilbao in the distance, its collection of decrepit buildings illuminated by the slanted sun. A barge was making its way across the river, ferrying cars it had picked up from the other side. "There they go again," Bjorn teased Simone, nodding at the two men operating the barge. They were muscled men in their late twenties with windblown hair and sun-browned faces. By their striking resemblance to each other, I presumed they were brothers. The men had scrambled up in front for a closer look at Simone.

"They've got it in for you, Simone," Elena kidded. Everyone knew Simone as an inveterate flirt but nothing would have prepared us for what she did next. She stripped off her dress and stretched out on the jetty only in her panties, imitating Marilyn Monroe's notorious calendar pose. "Simone, what are you doing?" Allison protested.

"Shhh. Just watch and see." The brothers were now

clawing at each other for a better look at Simone and not paying attention to their navigating. To our horror, the barge began to swing at a dubious angle, heading straight at the concrete pier that protruded out to the river.

"Cuidado! Cuidado! Watch out for the pier!" Elena cried out in alarm, pointing at the barge's nose. The brothers, seeing their mistake, yelped an obscenity and yanked at the steering wheel. The barge swerved sharply and at the last second slipped into the dock with barely an inch to spare. It banged against the retaining wall, bounced back with the impact, and stopped, jiggling the cars on board. Curses of consternation burst out of the passengers as they angrily gunned their engines.

"See what you did," Allison reprimanded Simone who had now turned sickly pale as she tried to get into her dress. It was only by a stroke of luck that no one was injured. Still muttering to each other, the brothers opened the gate to let the vehicles through, and when the last of them had rumbled out and the gate had been retracted, the stockier of the two men crossed the wooden plank and approached Simone with determination. Simone paled even more and cast me a beseeching glance. I stood up, as did Bjorn.

The man halted in front of Simone and exclaimed, "Ah Signorina, you are so beautiful we almost had an accident," he said with an Italian accent. Bjorn and I glanced at each other.

"When you took off your camisa, pooof, I thought I was going to die," the man tapped his forehead and made a theatrical gesture with his hand. Recovering her composure, Simone huffed, "Well, be more careful the next time." As if she didn't start the whole thing.

"Perdoname , signorina. Let me make it up to you." At this he grabbed her hand and genuflected in front of her. "That was our last trip for the day, my brother Marco and I. Por favor, let me take you and your friends for a ride on our barge.

"You want us to ride in that thing?" Simone replied indignantly.

"Oh no-no-no, not this one signorina. Another one, no? A much nicer barco. We have vino and tapas on board. We will entertain, si?"

Simone looked at us, and we all shrugged. What the heck, we had nothing better to do. A trip down the river wouldn't be so bad.

The brothers were named Fausto and Marco. I could tell by their rugged appearance that they spent a considerable amount of time working outdoors, for their faces, while not homely, were leathery and creased with deep lines along the forehead and mouth and their hands, calloused and huge, were rougher than the coarsest sandpaper. Fausto was the stockier of the two and the younger. It was obvious that they both wanted Simone and were competing for her attention.

We piled into the barge with more ebullience than we had originally shown. After all, we had never seen Bilbao from the vantage point of the river.

"Where did you say this boat is?" Allison asked Fausto.

"It is a kilometer down the river, signorina. In the next town." Fausto gunned the engine.

For ten bobbing minutes, we coasted along the Nervion, avoiding the ducks amassed around us, a tricky maneuver considering there were thousands of them. But we came out of it without killing too many. At length, Fausto slipped the boat into a private pier at Baracaldo along which were docked other barges of the same manufacture, each one of them looking alike.

The boat of which he spoke was a replica of the barge, but considerably smaller, with a funky wooden structure in the middle that served as the living quarters. The house had two stories. The top floor had a flat roof that doubled as a deck around which was a wrought iron railing. I could see a weathervane sticking out of the railing, capped by what looked like grillwork of a flying duck, obviously an influence of the famed Nervion ducks.

The main floor was surrounded by planter boxes, not of wood, but of concrete painted a bright periwinkle blue on which grew purple and yellow pansies and an assortment of plants and flowers. A golden retriever was loose on the deck, woofing enthusiastically at our approach.

"We live here," Marco said, jumping onto the boat's platform. The boat made a gentle thud and came to a complete stop.

"But where did you get it?" Allison asked.

"Ah signorina, my brother and I, we build boats. Good boats. These houseboats around us, we built all of them. And the barge too that takes the cars across the river. It is what we do."

Marco bent down to pet the dog. It swept the floor with its tail.

"How cute. What's his name?" Elena asked.

"Benito. For Benito Mussolini."

"Mussolini!" Simone scoffed. "How could you name him

after that horrible man."

"Oh no-no, signorina. It is a joke name, yes? Mussolini, he is like a dog—he is worse than a dog."

The interior of the house was as funky as its exterior. The walls were swathed in Moorish drapery of vermilion, gold, and brown pattern effectively blocking out the sun that would have been seeping through the picture windows. A sunken den sat in the middle of the room plump with Turkish rugs and pillows, and behind it, a bar with mahogany wall shelvings filled with liquor bottles, snifters, and what looked like a brass water pipe with a looping mouthpiece. To the right of the sunken den climbed a spiral staircase leading to the second floor, and still farther on towards the aft, a self-contained kitchen with an exit door to the side.

I followed Elena to the second floor, and came upon a narrow hallway with a bedroom on each side, both open, both dark, both embellished in the same Moorish draperies. Incense reeked; jasmine would be my guess. A step ladder of blackened steel rose up to the ceiling leading to the roof deck.

We climbed to the deck and watched a wooden barge chug out of the harbor. From our vantage point, we had a panoramic view of the river. Below us, we could see Bjorn inspecting the flower beds, and Allison and Marco at the navigation wheel. Fausto and Simone were nowhere to be found.

"Isn't this nice?" Elena said, leaning on the deck railing.

"Yeah. Very." I watched Allison with Marco in front of the barge. Each day that passed increased my longing for her. Sometimes, the feeling got so intense I was actually afraid.

"She is some woman, isn't she?" Elena said softly.

"Yes...she is."

"When she first arrived, I never thought we would be this close," Elena said. "Now, she is like a sister to me. Especially after you two became friends." She nudged me on the arm. "Do you love her?"

I shrugged. I didn't know if it was love but the feeling was close to it.

"She may be waiting for you, you know."

I shook my head. "She is too beautiful for me, Elena. Anyway, she has Francisco."

"Francisco? Are you kidding? I wouldn't trade five of him for one of you."

I hugged her around the waist. "Thanks for the vote of confidence, Elena. You're such a friend."

"Well, what I say stands. Frankly, I think she's in love with you."

I tried to smile but couldn't. If only it were true.

"Anyway," she continued, "this is between you and Allison. Francisco has nothing to do with it. And if he offers you a little competition, so much the better. Then you would really know."

I turned to her and smiled. Of my roommates, Elena was the only person I could talk to in a straightforward way. She never minced words.

When the barge was well into the river, we decided to join the others. Taking the flight of stairs down to the living room, we stepped into the landing, and pulled up short. There on the sunken den, half naked and moaning, lay Simone. She was engaged in a passionate embrace with Fausto who at that moment, had hiked up her dress and was fondling her inner thigh. Her breasts, large and milky white spilled out of her unbuttoned front, nipples distended. Fausto feasted on them.

We stared at them in disbelief, feeling an awkward embarrassment at this raunchy display of sex, and as we backed out of the room mortified, I couldn't help but feel a certain amount of arousal, for up until that time, I never really thought of my roommates as potential sexual partners, not even Allison who I had placed at an unattainable pedestal. But now, that imaginary glass had been shattered. Anything was possible.

When we rejoined the others, Elena said, "Quite a place you have here, Marco." She gave me a knowing glance and rolled her eyes. Bjorn came over and joined us. He had a curious expression on his face. He jerked a thumb at the planter boxes. "Is that marijuana growing over there?"

"Si, señor. But only for medicinal purposes," Marco said. "Ah por Dios, I think I'm feeling ill already," he added dramatically, whereupon he pulled out a ruby-studded brass cigarette case and flipped the lid open. Red, white, and green cigarettes filled the compartment.

"Ah let's see," Marco said. "Which one is for love sickness? Ah si, the red one." He turned to Allison. "You have love sickness, yes? " Allison glanced at me with her big round eyes and quickly looked away, blushing. Marco handed the joint to her.

I hadn't smoked grass in a long time, having given it up as a juvenile activity. But we were in Spain and the night was young so I took a few puffs. Immediately, my eyes grew heavy. I was drawn into a mild stupor.

I walked around the deck to the boat's stern and watched the Deusto Bridge slowly become smaller. I could see our apartment building in the distance with the fourth floor windows lit up. Cliff and Miguel must've returned from their weekend trip to Plencia.

I became aware of Allison standing next to me. She was so close I could feel her body heat along the side of my arm. I caught a whiff of her fragrance, a clean soapy smell, so sweet, so fresh, like fresh lilacs.

We stood in pensive silence, waiting for the other to initiate the conversation. "A penny," she said after a while.

"We've been here three months," I said.

She nodded. "Time flies so fast. Sometimes I wish I could stop it." She gave a nervous laugh. "If I had that power, you know when I would?"

"When?"

"When we were eating lunch at the park. I was so happy then."

It was the most wonderful thing she had ever said to me. "Thanks Allison," I said, genuinely touched. I looked at her. Tears threatened her eyes.

"What's the matter?" I asked gently.

She shook her head. "It's just that sometimes I feel I'm hurting you and I don't know why."

I touched her arm. "You're not hurting me, Allison. You do what you do because it's you. I wouldn't want it any other way."

"I'm sorry I turned sappy." She wiped a tear away.

"Nothing to be sorry about. I do it all the time." I smiled. Then gently, "How long are you staying?"

"Through August. I have to be back in school by September 5." Her voice quavered. "I never thought it would be like this, Jaime," she said.

"Things happen for a good reason, Allison."

Her grip tightened around the railing and she looked straight ahead. "Not always. Sometimes they happen for the wrong reasons."

Her bitterness took me by surprise. "What do you mean?"

She just shook her head. And as if to change the subject, she said, "What about you?"

"I'm not going back."

She didn't say anything.

I felt I needed to explain. "I can't go back, Allison."

"But why?"

I looked out in the distance, pondering whether or not to tell her. I had kept it inside me all these months. "Something happened before I left Manila, " I said finally. I glanced at her. "Ever wonder why I arrived in Bilbao early?"

"It was a little odd. But I thought you just wanted to brush up on your Spanish. Except you already spoke it quite well."

I nodded. My hands gripped the metal bar. "About a month before I was to leave for my traineeship, my mom asked me to chaperone my sister to a class party."

"Class party?"

"Yeah. That's what we call it. You see, schools in Manila are not coed. They're mostly either all boys or all girls. At least the private ones. So to socialize, the schools often hold joint parties. The girls' high school class is often matched with the guys' college class."

Allison looked at me doubtfully, but remained quiet.

"Anyway, we hold these parties at a classmate's house. We normally pick the biggest one at an exclusive part of town. My sister's party was at a mansion in Forbes Park. That's where all the millionaires live. This house was really huge with tennis courts and everything. Nothing really happens at these parties, you know. They're pretty tame. I've gone to hundreds of them.

"We talk, we dance, and later, we exchange phone numbers. Pretty innocent stuff. That night, I saw my sister dancing with this guy Pancho. He's the son of a three-star general. I didn't think much of it. I mean, the guy was nice looking and well-behaved. Went to a good school. I just didn't think anything could happen.

"Anyway, I got to talking to this girl, my sister's classmate actually. We danced a few times, had some punch. When I looked back to check on my sister, she was gone.

"At first, I wasn't worried. I thought they just went out for fresh air or something. But I was her chaperone and I promised my mom. So I went outside to check anyway. I snooped around the tennis courts and the garden, thinking they might be taking a walk. When I didn't find them there, I began to get worried.

"I went around to the other side of the property, and that's when I heard her cries coming from the greenhouse." I closed my eyes and tried to remember what happened. I had blocked it for so long. "I found them inside. My sister's clothes were all torn up and she was bleeding through the nose. This—this guy Pancho was on top of her with his hands around her neck. I—I just lost it. I grabbed him by the hair and dragged him away from Marina. He started swinging at me and things got out of hand." I shook my head. "I picked up a rock and smashed it into his face."

Allison gasped.

"The guy ended up in a hospital with a fractured skull."

"Were you charged?"

"Of course not. I was defending my sister. He's the one who should be in jail. In the Philippines, rape is a capital offense. Worse than murder." I shook my head. "But the guy will never be punished. His family is too powerful."

"But why can't you go home?"

"His father is a powerful general. He's got this private army and is the suspected leader of a death squad. My cousin said they'll never leave me alone. He's a captain in the military. He said I'll disappear just like those other people."

We were silent for a moment. Fearing her reaction to violence, I couldn't bring myself to look at her.

"But what are you going to do?" she asked in a worried voice.

I let out a frustrated breath. "I don't know. But don't worry, I'll figure something out. I always have."

"Jaime, you're my friend. Of course I worry about you." She touched my arm. "I'll always be there for you, Jaime. If you need to talk...have someone around...just let me know." She stared into my eyes. "Even if I'm with friends. I mean it."

I nodded. That word again. Friend. Is that all I was to her? A friend? Or was there something more.

"Promise me," she pressed.

"I promise."

I put an arm around her waist, felt her stiffen momentarily. Then slowly, she relaxed. We stood there for a long time, lost in each other's thoughts. My heart ached to draw her in, shower her with kisses, but I didn't have the nerve to do so. I was getting too many mixed signals.

When we walked back to join the others, we found them gathered in front, pointing at the shadowed cliffs that dominated the landscape. Fausto had meandered out of the house sporting a euphoric look.

"Where's Simone?" I asked.

"La signorina is touring the house," Fausto said, lighting the obligatory cigarette. He wiped the sweat from his forehead. While no one was looking, he stole a glance at Marco. A knowing smile passed between them; the briefest of nods towards the house. Oh-oh, I thought. Poor Simone is about to get a double whammy.

As I watched Marco sneak his way in, I wondered if the brothers derived unusual pleasure in sharing their conquests in this fashion. It seemed awfully kinky to me. But even as I was musing over this, a sicker thought crept into my mind: What would it feel like making love to a woman who had just been devoured by another man. I shook off the thought. I didn't want to get any crazy ideas about being the third in line.

I turned to Fausto. "Where are we going anyway?"

"To Cachondo. It's thirty kilometers downriver where the Nervion joins up with Biscay."

"Cachondo," Elena said. "What a strange name."

"Why would anyone name a town like that?" Bjorn asked.

"Ah, but there is a story behind it, señor. A good one. Legend has it that in 1875, a caravan of French Gypsies passed through the town when it was nothing more than a stable."

"But I thought Gypsies in Spain come from Andalusia?" Bjorn said.

Fausto rolled his eyes. "Gypsies come from everywhere señor. They come from France, from Germany, from England, and even Eastern Europe and Asia. They are nomads. They don't have real places to live. Especially in those times. Anyway, this tribe was led by a man named Miro Cachondo."

"The king of the Gypsies?" I asked.

"Eso es, señor. Cachondo was the chieftain of a Manouche tribe. And like a king, he had everything. He had a beautiful wife named Papillona, a trusted friend named Moritz, and a good herd of horses. What more could a Gypsy want?

"On the surface, everything seemed fine. Cachondo's tribe had three successful years selling horses in Andalusia and his people were happy. But in this particular year, they decided to go south with an even bigger herd thinking of doubling their money.

"They threw everything they had into that pilgrimage. It was a big gamble on their part but if it paid off, it would sustain them for years to come. Anyway, Cachondo didn't know that behind his back, Papillona and Moritz were cheating on him and planning something nefarious. Every night when Cachondo had fallen asleep, Papillona would slip out of their marriage bed and sneak into Moritz's tent to engage in carnal love. Papillona and Moritz were two of a kind, you see. Lust and greed ruled their minds. She would stay in Moritz's tent for hours and do all sorts of lurid things with him then sneak back into Chachondo's tent before dawn." Fausto swung the barge to avoid another wave of river ducks.

"I can't believe Cachondo would sleep through that every night," Elena said.

"Ah, but signorina, they were poisoning him. From the

time they crossed the Pyrenees, Papillona had been sprinkling dried cowdung and poisonous herbs on his food."

"Dried cowdung?" Allison made a face.

"Si, it is very bad. The poison made him ill. So ill in fact that by the time they reached San Sebastian, Cachondo was vomiting blood. For three weeks, they poisoned him and for three weeks he vomited. He was relieving himself ten-twenty times a day. His people didn't know what was wrong with him, and they never suspected that Papillona and Moritz had anything to do with his condition. In any event, by the time the caravan arrived in Vizcaya, Cachondo had slipped into a coma. That was when his people thought their poor king was going to die."

The swarm of ducks abated and he swung the barge towards the middle of the river.

"But they had a dilemma, you see. What are they going to do with him? On one hand, he was hampering their progress because of the constant delays dictated by his deteriorating health. As it was, they only had a few weeks to make it to the horse fair at Jaranquez, which meant they had to travel double time. But on the other hand, Cachondo was already dying and probably had only a few days to live, if at all. So after much agonizing on their part and encouragement from Moritz who professed to have the best interest of the tribe at heart, they decided to leave him."

"You mean they'd just abandon their king?" Allison protested.

"He was dying, signorina. And to the Gypsies, the annual pilgrimage is a holy rite. It also meant survival. Their till at Andalusia would support them in the winter months. If they didn't make the horse fair, they would starve.

"So in preparation for his death, they built him a shrine. A death tent, if you will. They ladened it with food and stored his belongings in it. Then they picked his personal horses from the herd and lashed them onto a makeshift stable outside the tent."

"What for? He was dying anyway," Elena, ever practical, said.

Fausto shook his head. "Gypsies are superstitious people, signorina. It was an offering to the heavens to help him in his final journey. It was the least they could do for a chieftain that had been so good to them."

"But the horses will die with him," Allison protested.

"As they should. Because if they didn't, his spirit would live with the horses and give the tribe bad luck. It is a Gypsy belief, signorina. In fact, they were supposed to set the death tent on fire, but of course, they couldn't do that because he was still alive."

"So, the bad people won," Bjorn said. His lips curled in disgust.

"Ah but Cachondo didn't die. Because without the poison, he was able to recover. He was as strong as a bull, you see. You couldn't kill him. In fact, he woke up from the coma after only a week. But he was so weak he could hardly sit up. He ate the food they left behind and drank the wine, and when that was all gone, he contemplated eating the horses."

"Yuch," Allison said.

"No signorina, horse meat is muy bueno, eh. You should try it."

Allison made a face.

"Anyway, Cachondo resisted eating the horses because they were a forbidden meat for the Gypsies. But he was tempted, and he kept looking at them longingly. Fortunately, on that very day, a large flock of ducks came down from the Vizcayan falls, filling up the entire expanse of the river. He knew then he was saved. For four weeks, he ate nothing but roast duck. The meat reinforced his muscles and the oil made him strong. Eventually, he was able to recover."

Fausto waved at the crew of a fishing boat making its way upriver. The net was still on its pulley and I could see a thick mass of fish wriggling inside it. When the boat had passed, Fausto continued, "Then one day, a freak storm blew in from the west. It was so ferocious it destroyed all the ships making their way through the Nervion. Of the fifteen ships that were destined for Bilbao, only three ships survived. The only problem was, the storm was so powerful it blew them into the riverbank.

"The Capitanes became desperate. Por Dios, they exclaimed, the ships are stuck. How are they going to ship the cargo to Bilbao? The whole city will starve."

"Weren't there other ships that could have pulled them out?" Bjorn challenged.

"What ships, amigo? They were all destroyed. Even if they weren't, the river was not passable because of the debris."

"So what happened next?"

"Cachondo offered his services to the capitanes. He said, 'Señores, I will carry your cargo over these mountains using my fine horses but for a handsome price.' At first, the capitanes balked on accepting the services of a mere Gypsy, especially at such an outrageous price. But seeing little choice in the matter, they eventually agreed.

"And so with his six horses, Cachondo trekked over the Vizcayan mountains loaded down with goods. The trip was grueling but Cachondo had Gypsy horses. They were big and strong and sure-footed, and Cachondo was able to make the delivery in only seven days.

"With his mission completed, Cachondo returned with horses and wagons, and cooks, and carpenters. He even brought along a crew of unemployed stevedores to cart the remainder of the goods to Bilbao. He became muy rico, yes? Very rich. He built a makeshift hostel so that the ship's crew could sleep in comfortable quarters while they worked on the ships. He opened a restaurant so they could eat decent food, he even built a bar so they could drink good wine. And that was how the town started.

"Ever since then, the Cachondo trail became known to the Gypsies as the Camino De La Buena Suerte or the Goodluck Trail. Gypsies from all over Europe pass through there every year."

Bjorn said, "But what happened to the bad Gypsies? Moritz and what's her name..."

"Papillona. After the horse fair, they stole the Gypsy coffer and took off for Morocco with all the money. But they didn't stop their plotting and stealing."

"Que mal," Elena said.

"My sentiments exactly. It is in their blood, signorina. But do not despair because one day, it finally caught up with them. They were arrested for robbing an Arab prince after Papillona seduced him and fed him her poisonous herbs. Unfortunately for them, the prince died of a heart attack while in bed with

Papillona. They were blamed for it."

Bjorn nodded in satisfaction. Justice had finally been served. "I bet they sent them to jail and threw away the keys."

"Oh no, señor. It is more serious than that. You now have a dead prince, you see. An entirely different story. At noon of the next day, the palace guards marched Papillona and Moritz into the town square to be tried by the masses. Everyone in Marrakesh attended. Hundreds of them.

"Guilty! the townspeople clamored. Death to the Gypsies! Being a woman, Papillona was to go first. They took her from her stake kicking and screaming, and even with her hands lashed behind her back, it took three men to drag her to the tree stump."

"Jesus, what are they going to do with her?" Bjorn said.

"Jesus is the right word, señor, because he was the only one that could've saved her that day," Fausto said.

"After much effort, one man pulled at her hair and forced her head onto the stump cheek flush against the surface, while another man sat on her legs so she couldn't struggle.

"It was at this point that the executioner marched into the square with his gleaming scimitar." Fausto's voice lowered to a whisper. "He was bald and bearded with ropes of muscles on his arms. But it was the eyes that made Papillona gasp because in them she saw the glint of death. She began to scream. Loud, piercing screams, like that of a wounded animal. Por favor, por favor, I didn't do it, I didn't do it, she pleaded. But to no avail. Finally, the moment of justice came. The executioner touched the sharp edge of the blade onto her neck and Papillona began to whimper. With both hands, the executioner lifted the sword, stared down Papillona's veined neck, and savagely brought it down."

Bjorn groaned.

"Papillona's head flew off, bouncing and rolling in the dust with the grimace still on it. They said she had so desperately wanted to escape the executioner's sword that her headless body flapped around like a chicken before it became still."

"What happened to the Gypsies?" Elena asked. A ferry boat motored by and rocked our barge.

"Calamitous things happened to them, signorina. They journeyed back to Northern France as they had been doing for hundreds of years but were ill-prepared to face the harsh winter. Without money, they couldn't buy food so they starved. Some of the children died. It was the longest winter they had ever had. Mercifully, spring came, and with it a promise of a new life. They once again embarked on their journey south, a bedraggled, pathetic group. They passed the town of Cachondo which by then had prospered into a booming port. Cachondo saw them coming down from the mountain; he saw their ragged appearance and wept. His poor tribe, how they had suffered."

"How sad," Allison said.

"Yes. But at least he could do something about it. He had a lot of money now, you see. He felt that he must lead them again to give them a better life. He sold all his properties in town and rejoined the caravan. So there you have it, the legend of Cachondo."

Allison and Elena clapped their hands. "What a wonderful story."

"It is a true story, signorinas."

They gave him a dubious look. I knew they didn't believe a

word of it, particularly Elena who was hard-nosed about most things to begin with. It wasn't until much later that night that Fausto got his vindication.

"There it is now," Fausto said, pointing at the shimmering lights of the town. Evening had set in and the sky had become a deep sable. I could see the ragged outline of the rooftops juxtaposed against the mountains. Several ships were on port, their decks ablaze with lights. Switching off the engine, Fausto angled the barge towards the quay, coasting it expertly between two fishing boats. A group of sailors waved at us from the platform.

"Bueno, vamonos," Fausto said as the barge made the compulsory bump and remained still. I went inside the house to fetch Simone and was greeted by the sound of squeaking box springs. Above me, a headboard banged against the wall, competing with passionate cries of fornication, and for a few racy seconds, I was tempted to go upstairs and peek. But that would have been a bit too kinky. Oh well, I thought, as I stepped out into the night and hurried to catch up with the rest of the party.

☼ 10 Night Dancers

Cachondo was like any other town along the river: carved on a cliff, clustered with ramshackle houses, and sectioned by slender passageways. Its streets were steep and hard to walk on by virtue of their uneven surface. There were no pavements in the entire town, only wet slippery cobblestones.

I crossed a large parking lot that served as the loading dock for the merchant ships, and puffed my way up a winding street that seemed to have no end. Much of the bars in town spilled with people, and it was not unusual even at this early hour for me to encounter a man or two already reeling from the effects of alcohol.

I spotted my friends near a crest in the hill, struggling to make the grade with Fausto playing the role of a tourist guide, vigorously motioning at the various points of interest in town, and as I caught up with them at the summit, I noticed that we had entered an elegant looking park bordered by a neat row of cypress trees that had been pruned into perfect candlelights, and of it, I can say only this: it was one of the more impressive parks I had ever seen in that it was so serene it reminded me of a painting I once saw in Bilbao; *Une Bagne* by Georges Seurat. Although there was a conflux of people in the park, as parks usually had during this time of day, I didn't sense an urgency in them that would later manifest itself. I noticed the usual things: couples on evening promenades, a man seated on a bench, an old lady walking a dog, a dog barking at a cat, a cat arching its back.

Fausto herded us to El Marisco, a bar in which the local fishermen congregated. It was not your usual town bar, for this one was indeed a true fisherman's haunt as the nets on the floor, still wet from the ocean haul attested; I could see grimy rubber boots, shiny wet slickers, and tattered seaman's caps in one corner of the room neatly arranged in rows and stacks so that they wouldn't get in the way of drinking. Bursts of laughter punctuated the air. Not surprisingly, Fausto knew everyone in the room, calling out an *Hola* here and a *Que tal* there, engaging every now and then in a frisky exchange of long distance ribbing.

They were a roughhewn lot with large calloused hands and dark stubbled faces many of whom showed the telltale signs of painful windburn. All stunk of the ocean. A group of stevedores, faces flushed from sun and alcohol, were gathered around a corner table belting out a rendition of Tiriki Trauki, a popular Basque ballad whose melody I had heard so many times in Bilbao, except that this troupe's rendition of it didn't sound anything like the touching ballad I knew because of their horrific drunken voices.

"Oye Italiano, I see you brought some friends with you," a burly man with a striped sweater shouted from the bar.

"Yes, they are extranjeros from the university," Fausto announced.

"Come on, bring them over. I want to meet them."

Even though at times Spaniards utter the word extranjero with a hint of contempt, they are nevertheless fascinated by them and truly enjoy their company. It was not unusual for a foreigner to be approached by a complete stranger and be invited for a drink or some tasty tapa, for such was the hospitality of the Spaniard.

"Ven, ven," Fausto said. "Let me introduce you to my friend Capitan Olivares."

Capitan Olivares as it turned out was not really a captain but a retired seaman who had traveled just about every nook and cranny of this earth, which was precisely the reason why they allowed him the honorary title of Capitan. To my astonishment, he even knew the tiny village I grew up in.

"Phil-Am Village!" he exclaimed. "In Manila. Yes, I was there in '76. Do you know Ditas Conejo?" How he knew Ditas Conejo, the town prostitute, I had no way of knowing but he was able to describe every detail about the woman, including her most private anatomy, which I didn't care to hear.

Although only forty-five, Olivares was forced to retire from sailing when a crateload of steel rods bound for the freeways of Bilbao fell off the crane. The impact of the fall shattered the crate and sent the deadly rods spearing across the deck. Olivares, who had taken whitewash duty that morning in lieu of a day in town, was leaning over the railing with a brush when he saw the deadly spears coming in his direction. He barely had time to yelp. A rod gouged his shoulder and another one, his leg. The force of the blows were so powerful it knocked him off the boat and into the river, and it was only through the good graces of fate that he didn't sink because the rods got trapped in between the wooden columns of the pier.

They had to fish him out of the water and rush him to a hospital with the rods still attached to him. The story had it that it took five doctors four hours to extricate him from the rods with the help of such unscientific tools as a blow torch, an electric saw, and a wrench.

"Mira," Olivares said later, opening his shirt to show us the scar. Allison grimaced and looked away. The scar was so sunken and so large it looked like the depression of a fist. I noticed that while his left arm was bulging with muscles, his right one was withered and deformed with hardly any meat on the bone.

"Oye Arturo, trae me los cangrejos. Ladle me some crawfish," Olivares bellowed to the bartender. The bartender, a wizened old man with a missing tooth, nodded to him briskly, picked up a large bowl from the counter, and filled it with a generous helping of tomatoed crawfish.

Playing the hospitable host, Olivares pushed the overflowing bowl to our faces and made us sample the dish. Bjorn inspected it doubtfully.

"Venga! Toma!" Olivares insisted. "Son muy bueno."

Everyone dipped into the bowl and fished out a crawfish. From what I could taste, there was some garlic in the brew and a trace of cayenne pepper and onion. And while it was admittedly delicious, it was also hard to eat; one had to do a lot of sucking to get even an inch of meat—hardly worth the trouble and the mess.

Simone and Marco entered the bar and everyone gave them a knowing look. Simone, her face flushed and glowing, had a contented cast about her that was almost sedate, not unlike someone who had just come out of a massage parlor. Of all the people I met in Spain that year, she was the only one who was completely at peace with her sexuality and I envied her for it. It would have helped those of us who traveled to Andalusia later that summer deal with the lure of the flesh.

We were on our second glass of wine and dipping into more crawfish when a bearded seaman barreled through the door. "They're coming! They're coming!"

All of a sudden, everyone was jumping out of his seat.

"What's going on?" I asked Marco.

"The Gypsies—they've arrived," he said excitedly. "Come, come, let's have a look." We all filed into the street and stood looking around the park. At first I didn't see them. I only heard the neighing of many horses and the rumble of many cars. Then they appeared around the bend; a whole caravan of them on ox-drawn carts and motorized trailers. They came in a blaze of light and music. As they approached the park, the lead wagon, a big wooden cart with a white canvas top, halted and let out six Gypsies, all of whom carried fiddles and accordions and wore colorful flowing costumes. They sported elaborately embroidered vests and generously ruffled dresses, and always with glittering jewelry. They danced around the street, playing a strange blend of music that was both Latin and Arabic. Like Greek or Italian polka. And as the first wagon proceeded around the park, a second one took its place, letting out yet another batch of performers, this time in colorful tights, quite unlike a Gypsy costume, but more like those worn by circus performers.

They were young and lithe and bursting with energy. The women wore red and green tights accentuated by purple masks while the men wore electric blue highlighted with crimson sashes. They pranced around the park in a riot of colors, doing difficult somersaults and handstands. They dove through blazing hoops and twirled fiery batons. I gorged on the visual rhapsody, unable to believe my eyes.

Each wagon that followed let out another batch of performers until the entire park, in a matter of minutes, was buzzing with them. There were fortune tellers, magicians, acrobats, and clowns, and amidst all these razzle-dazzle were teenage Gypsy girls working the crowd to collect donations. One of them, a dark-haired girl of about seventeen approached me with an aluminum can. She made a riveting sight, for not only was she beautiful, but also gloriously exotic, with jet black hair, large dark eyes, and the bronziest of skin. She was wearing a sleeveless white blouse, a red skirt, and a pair of green espadrilles. On her neck were strands of gold and around her wrists, matching bangles. I pulled out a fifty peseta coin and dropped it in the coffer. "Gracias," she said with a smile.

The caravan had now encircled the park and the night took on a carnival atmosphere. I searched around for my friends but I seemed to have lost them in the tumult. I spotted Allison in a small circle of people in front of what looked like an oversized striped wagon. I approached curiously.

"What's going on?" I asked.

"Flamenco," she said, nodding towards the dancers and

musicians in the middle of the gathering. She seemed hypnotized by their movements. "...Suena la Margarita con sus romeros..." the musicians wailed. *The Dream of Marguerite*, a song about a beautiful woman and her seven lovers.

The dancers, two men and a woman, stomped their feet impetuously, clacking resonant castanets. Their faces were a grimace of fervid lines. One man stood out: a dashing young Gypsy in a red bolero jacket and glittering green sash. He was, without a doubt, the best dancer of the group and seemed to have captivated the onlookers that had now grown in number. "Aupa Montalvo," the musicians exhorted.

The crowd massed around the trio, clapping their hands in encouragement. There was something primitive about the dance that drew me, like a taste of a forbidden fruit, a release of a hidden passion that was both intoxicating and reckless. At once, the dancers began taking women from the crowd and dancing with them.

I saw Allison pulled into the circle by the Gypsy named Montalvo. She danced rather well, even for an extranjero. She stomped with the expertise of a native and threw her head back like a Gypsy. I was impressed.

When Montalvo brought her back to me, she was flushed with excitement. It was at this time that I saw something that made me wary. My eyes riveted upon a couple on the opposite side of the circle who at first glance appeared perfectly normal until you keyed in on the man's eyes and realized they were out of kilter. Unkempt and obviously intoxicated, he was watching the dance with open hostility, clenching and unclenching his fists every now and then to show his agitation. I had been in Spain long enough to recognize the first sign of a pelea or a fight, and that, coupled with the knowledge that many Spaniards viewed Gypsies with disdain was enough to draw my caution. I began to watch this man, for whatever mischief he had in mind could easily spark a riot, especially in this highly charged atmosphere.

I inched closer to Allison, ready to grab her if anything were to happen. It came to me that what really bothered the man even more than the dancing Gypsies was his girlfriend's obvious fascination with them. I remembered the frozen grin on the woman's face as she watched the oscillating dance, how she tapped her feet with the music. Then the heckling began. The man called the Gypsies unmentionable names both in Spanish and in French, and even though his girlfriend tried to calm him down, he continued with his tirade. Like a raging lunatic, he shook his fists at them.

Perhaps out of embarrassment at the blatant display of prejudice or simply to prove a point to her idiot of a boyfriend, the woman left his side and began dancing with Montalvo. She was a good dancer and they became quite a pair. The audience started clapping and more people gathered to watch, drowning out the man's heckling. In one fluid movement, the Gypsy twirled the woman around, dunking her by the waist to the obvious glee of the crowd.

Suddenly, I heard a loud curse. To my horror, I saw the man charging towards the Gypsy with something long and sharp in his hand. I cried out a warning, diving into the circle to push the Gypsy aside. But my efforts came too late. The man was already upon him, plunging the knife deep into the Gypsy's chest. The girlfriend screamed. People gaped at the unexpected violence. For a brief second, the Gypsy pirouetted on tiptoes, his face etched in disbelief. He staggered back, clutching his chest. A froth of blood bubbled out of his mouth. Then with an anguished cry, he collapsed on the pavement.

Allison screamed and bedlam erupted. A gang of men tackled the boyfriend to the ground, twisting at his knifehand. I darted to the wounded man whose body was being racked by violent convulsions. With my hands, I tried to stem the tide gushing out of his chest, but it was like containing a surging river. Blood squirted through my fingers, shooting up on my arms and face. God, don't let him die on me, I muttered. His eyes glazed over. He gave one last twitch, then lay still.

Frantically, I pumped on his chest, more out of frustration than of hope. I blew air into his mouth not knowing whether he was still breathing. Someone touched my shoulder but I roughly shook it off. I didn't know what had gotten into me. It was as though I were possessed. "Esta muerto, he's dead," they kept telling me but I was unable to stop. I became aware of the Gypsy girl to whom I had given the fifty pesetas kneeling beside me. She cried out Montalvo's name.

I was still pumping and giving resuscitation when the paramedics dragged me away. I stopped and bowed my head, knowing I had failed. By then, a large crowd had gathered around us. I was vaguely aware of the boyfriend being carted off by the police and the Gypsy girl weeping by her fallen friend.

Allison took my arm and walked me to a fountain. Something tasted salty and I found myself spitting it out. I didn't know what was happening. I was living in a dream and watching myself from the sidelines at the same time. As Allison washed my hands, I stood in catatonic stupor, my eyes transfixed on the red eddy swirling around the drain. My shoulders shook and my teeth began to rattle. Perhaps out of pity or perhaps out of love, Allison took me in her arms.

"I—I'm sorry for acting this way," I said dazedly. "I—I didn't mean to be hysterical."

Allison had tears in her eyes. "You were wonderful, Jaime. You tried to save him when no one else would. You've got the biggest heart in the world." When she had cleaned me up, she kissed me on the cheek, took my arm, and walked me along the cobblestones towards the barge.

☼ 11 Of Love and War

Allison asked me a strange question. She asked why I reacted the way I did when the man stabbed the Gypsy. "So unlike you," she said. "You've always been a calm person."

I couldn't give her an answer. Frankly, I didn't know. It was no different than my actions in Manila the night Marina was violated; the overwhelming flash of emotion, the uncontrollable rage. The calm and the storm packaged in one skin. It was a flaw. It frightened me sometimes.

Two days had passed. I was strolling home after a bout of serious writing at the harbor when someone called out my name. It was ten o'clock and inky dark except for the subdued light filtering forth from the Cerveceria.

"Jaime," the call came again, barely audible in the distance. I squinted in the gloom trying to see who it was and saw two figures waving at me from the deep recesses of the trees. I approached curiously as the voice sounded like a woman's. It was only when I was ten meters away and well into the maze of tables that I made out the shadowed forms of Allison and Elena seated under a cottonwood tree. They watched me approach grinning broadly from the lamplight on their table, and I must tell you that they had to be the loveliest pair of unescorted young ladies in Bilbao that night, for not only were they dressed chicly in slick black mini dresses, but also quite made up. It was the first time I had seen Allison with rouge on, the effect of which made her look bewitching.

"We thought it was you," Allison greeted. She crossed her legs. "Been doing some writing?"

I nodded. She knew about the diary and my letters to Marina.

"Anything about me?" She pulled out a chair and patted the armrest.

"Always, my dear," I said, slumping into the seat next to her.

A smile crossed her face.

"And what might you gorgeous ladies be doing here all alone?" I surveyed them from head to toe. "And all dolled up."

"Oh, we were just about to have a drink," Elena said.

No sooner had she said that when I noticed the absence of drinks on the table. They're on a date, I thought. And as I glanced around the Cerveceria with a feeling of mortification creeping up inside, I saw to my dismay Francisco and Bjorn rounding up the drinks at the bar.

My immediate impulse was to leave; avoid a potentially delicate situation, but doing so would have been conspicuously awkward. Like an admission of jealousy; a shameful retreat.

Anyway, Allison begged me to stay, taking on one of those

pleading looks with raised eyebrows no self respecting man could refuse.

Against my better judgment, I stayed. After all, how bad could it be? I had never met Francisco, I had never talked to him, I had no opinion of him. Hell, he might turn out to be a nice guy.

But no sooner had he come to the table that it immediately became apparent he wasn't. That he had heard about me was obvious for he was fiercely opposed to my presence and showed it in a no nonsense way. He sat down on the other side of Allison, immediately staking his claim by wrapping an arm around her shoulders. And while I found the act to be laughably juvenile, it nonetheless did the trick. I found myself fuming inside.

"So, you're Jaime," he smirked.

"That's me," I parried. We measured each. He was about my height, 5'10 or 5'11 and of the same build. He looked like he kept in shape as much as I did, although I had never known Spaniards to be compulsive about such things. He had a fierce cast about him, not unlike a mountain lion on the prowl which made him look intimidating. His wealth of eyebrows made him doubly so.

They poured the beer but I didn't have a glass which underscored the fact that I was intruding. Allison took a sip of hers and passed it on to me. She began to look uncomfortable. As if to reinforce this point, she subtly disengaged Francisco's arm from her shoulders.

I saw a tightening in Francisco's jaw, but he quickly covered it up with a phony smile. Having won the first scrimmage, I piled it on. As the great generals advised, *Never give an inch. Divide and conquer.* And so I did.

I turned to Bjorn. "So buddy. Have you gotten over Elena's horror stories yet?" Bjorn's reaction to Elena's horrific Brazilian tales which she divvied to our group like rationed candies had become a private joke among us.

Bjorn snickered. "On the contrary, amigo, I'm beginning to have terrible nightmares about them. Did she tell you about the time her cousin Lucas was captured by the Amazons?"

Everyone burst out laughing, except for Francisco who didn't understand the joke. Strike two, I thought. By now, Francisco's smile had turned into a glower. His eyebrows thickened and fangs grew out of his mouth. He tried to stare me down. I returned it in spades. Once again, a frightening flash crept up on my face. His stare wavered.

"Well, I hate to poop out on you guys, but I really have to go." I pushed my chair back suddenly. "Tomorrow's another day with the bankers." I nodded to Francisco. "Encantado a conocerte."

He didn't return the nod.

I turned to Allison. "Thanks for the beer." Somehow, the words came out clipped. I was already at the riverwalk with my ears burning at the side of my head when a call came from behind me. "Jaime, Wait!"

I stopped, turned. It was Allison, face flushed and out of breath. I glanced at our table. Far and away but still clearly visible. "I'm sorry," she breathed. She put her arms around my neck and pulled me close. "I'll be home shortly. I promise," she whispered fiercely. Then with a peck on my lips, she turned and hastened back to the restaurant.

I gazed after her in confusion. Her actions caught me by

surprise. It was at this point that I realized that she had begun to commit herself to me. After months of hoping and praying and wishing for her love, it was finally happening.

I never saw her with Francisco after that.

☼ 12 The Fiesta

Senor Joacquin sauntered into my office in a gabardine suit, polka dot necktie, and gleaming slicked-back hair. "I have to go to San Sebastian for the day, Jaime. Why don't you take the afternoon off. I don't have anything for you to do anyway."

I looked at him doubtfully. Lately, he had been keeping erratic hours, taking off an hour here, a couple of hours there under the guise of 'taking care of business.' I began to suspect him of having an affair.

But I took him up on his offer. After all, it was Friday and it had been a while since I had a stroll around Bilbao.

I wandered for six blocks searching for a place to eat. The sun blazed overhead. I had just passed the department store El Corte Ingles when guess who I bumped into but lovely Allison coming out of its doors. Actually, I didn't see her, busy as I was looking at a Picasso etching at the display window of an art gallery.

"I thought you work Friday afternoons," she said from behind me.

I jerked up in surprise. "Allison. Jesus, you gave me a start." I regarded her appreciatively, noting her sleeveless peach dress with light pastel prints of wild roses complemented by a pair of Keds sneakers, no socks. She would have passed for a Vogue model if she hadn't been so voluptuous. "What are you doing here?" I asked.

"I'm off for the rest of the afternoon. I told my boss I had to run some errands."

We ended up having lunch in one of those blue collar eateries along the river where you could get a bowl of garbanzo soup, a plateful of steak and fries, a bottle of wine, a jug of gaseosa, and a pear for two hundred pesetas. Seagulls squawked outside the windows.

Allison ate like a bear fresh out of hibernation. She tore into the steak with gusto and chased it down with wine, and after a few minutes of knifing and chomping and decimating her food, she began to pick on mine, which was still a plateful. Gnawing on a piece of fry, she refilled our glasses. "Chin-chin," she said, raising her drink to me.

I took up mine and clinked it into hers. "Where in the world did you learn to eat like that?"

"From my mom. She eats like a horse. Funny thing is, she never grows fat. We had a contest once to see who can eat the most ice cream." She snickered. "My aunt, who was always on a diet got so mad she kicked us out of the room. I won the contest."

"And you never gain weight?"

"Nope. Never been on a diet in my life."

"Good match. Two people with high metabolism."

She blushed. There was a momentary lull. She gazed at me thoughtfully. "I've never met a man like you, Jaime."

"Hmmm, is that good or bad?"

She shrugged. A familiar expression sneaked up on her face. Was it worry? Fear? I began to wonder about it.

We strolled around the old part of Bilbao, window shopped at antique stores along the Casco Viejo, then took the train towards Deusto. Our stop came and went but we never got off. Sitting there together in the lulling drone of the train with our shoulders touching, it seemed like the thing to do.

"Hey, let's go to Algorda, want to?" Allison said after a while.

"Where's that?" I pretended to gaze out at the distant hills. Her arm grazed against mine.

"End of the line."

"But what's in Algorda?"

"A town. And a beach." She threw up her hands and giggled. "How the heck would I know. I've never been there before."

I smiled. "How far is it?"

From her purse, she pulled out a map and spread it on our laps. I leaned close, pretending to look. I smelled her hair.

"Do you like it?" she asked.

"Like what?"

"The smell of my hair."

"Oh—I'm sorry. I didn't mean to—"

She continued tracing the map, but didn't move away. Finally she said. "It's twenty miles."

The Band Of Gypsies

The train chugged on, snaking its way around the cliffs. We rumbled through several tunnels—dark, light, dark, light—made a final climb to the summit, and came to a grating stop at the terminal. The intercom blared. "Estacion de Algorda."

Algorda sat on a cliff overlooking the Sea of Cantabria. It was an enchanting little town with white cottages and cute little shops on very crooked streets. It had the atmosphere of a resort town, its sidewalks swept clean and lined with flowering magnolia trees except when you surveyed the people on the streets, you got the notion that they were locals; everybody seemed to know everyone else.

The town seemed to be preparing for a bash, for the townsfolk were stringing blue and orange banners along the sidewalks and securing them on trees and street lamps. Everywhere I turned I saw men in white costumes with plaid scarves tied around their necks.

Allison trotted over to a man supervising the stringing of the colored lights and asked him what was in the offing. The man, a wiry old geezer in a raspberry beret, plaid green kaiku jacket, and half length pantaloons declared, "Esta noche es la fiesta de Algorda."

He explained to us that tonight was the beginning of the fiesta honoring Algorda's patron saint San Miguel, a celebration that was to last three days and three nights, and as he spoke, I couldn't help but be mesmerized by the man, for he was indeed a feast for the eyes. His face was like a wind-battered cliff with cracks and crevices on the surface. His eyes were of the blackest color I had ever seen, perfect drops of black tar on pristine white retina, and his nose, noble and

Castilian, had a subtle hook to it that made him seem hawk-ish. But what really made him arresting in my eyes was the radiance of his personality which seemed to reach out and toy with my mind.

He must have been at least seventy but still bursting with energy. When I asked him about his costume, he tapped a dance and exclaimed, "Para el Baile de los Vascos. There will be a traditional Basque dance tonight and I will be there. It is a big celebration. Everyone will be dancing in the streets to launch off the fiesta." He motioned to us. "Come, come, let me show you around."

His name was Don Pedro Guidote, Tercero, the third Don Pedro in his family tree. He took us to every nook in town, from the old Algorda church with its cracked white bell tower and macabre gargoyle heads to the expansive brick plaza adjacent to the cliffs overlooking the Cantabria, all the while entertaining us with the town's colorful history. He swept an arm at the Vizcayan mountains. "During the peak of their reign, the Moors swept through the Basque country from the south and captured every town and city along the way. It was the only region of Spain they hadn't conquered, you see, and they wanted it desperately for its gold and silver.

"In the course of the invasion, there was a big battle at Burgos. Many men were killed, but the Basques, skilled at mountain fighting repelled the attackers and drove them back to the plains of Castille. The Moors couldn't get through by land so they tried invading by sea." Turning, he waved an arm at the Cantabria. "Anticipating the move, the Algordans mounted their catapults along the cliffs of Vizcaya to face the deadly invaders." His voice lowered into a whisper. "A ferocious battle ensued and the short supplied Algordans faced off with an incredible armada of ships. Out there on the horizon, they appeared, billowing fire and conflagration from their catapults. The Sea of Cantabria turned red with blood. Load after load, their catapults pounded the town, felling buildings, caving in walls. The sky darkened with streaking arrows. By the time it was over, only five ships remained but the Algordans were vanquished. The dead littered the streets."

We gaped at him, wanting to hear more.

"What happened to the townspeople?" Allison asked.

"The Moors swept in with their deadly scimitars. Amidst the fire and smoke, they flooded the streets swinging their mighty swords. Heads flew off and limbs were severed, and soon the entire town was awash in blood." He narrowed his eyes as if trying to recall the actual event. "They rounded up everybody—men, women, and children—lined them up against the wall, and slew them with their spears."

I was anxious to hear more but he straightened up suddenly. "Oh well, enough of this depressing story. Tonight, my family will have a celebratory party. All of my relatives will be there." He bowed gallantly. "I'd be honored if you came."

Allison took my hand and pressed it and before I could frame an answer, she said, "Yes, we will come."

"Very well, then. Las ocho. Eight o'clock." He gave us directions to his house, made a final bow, before bidding us adios.

After he left, I said, "Are you crazy? There's a new batch of interns arriving tonight. We're supposed to have dinner with them."

She waved a hand dismissively. "Inaki and the boys will do

fine without us."

She never let go of my hand. Since it was only seven, we took the flight of stairs down to the beach. It was a long trek on uneven steps without the benefit of guard rails such that by the time we were halfway down, I was sweating profusely, not of exertion but of fright.

But we made it down in one piece, thank God, as I had this fear of heights that was almost primeval, borne out of the fact that I fell from a guava tree once and knocked myself silly. Surprisingly, the beach was deserted, except for a few fishermen casting their lines at sea.

We wandered along the beach in silence, the first time we were truly alone together, far from Bilbao, far from our roommates, far from friends that could distract us. It was an experience ours to share, no one else, and we savored every minute of it. I didn't know what we had then but it was as close to a love affair as it could ever be. The sun was still up but low on the horizon. I could hear the surf pounding at the beach, creating wide ripples of foam in the sand. At the western tip of the shoreline, we rested at a cluster of boulders beyond which was another stretch of sand completely hidden from view, and here in this secluded spot, Allison led me to a boulder where we could watch the ocean or do whatever it was we wished to do without having to worry about being seen. What now, I thought.

With our heads side by side on the hard surface of the rock, we gazed out into the open sea. I took in her soapy fragrance eliciting in me a burning desire to take her in my arms. I sensed her watching me from the corners of her eyes but when I glanced at her, she was facing the sea.

"It's beautiful, isn't it?" she said softly. "Almost like a dream."

"Yes," I said. Once again, I felt inadequate as I wondered how a beautiful woman like her could fall for the likes of me. And yet here she was, holding my hand, waiting for me to make the move I was too paralyzed to make. Had it been any other woman, I would have had us rolling in the sand, humping furiously with our legs entangled. But with Allison, I was awestricken into immobility. And perhaps having ran out of patience, she finally faced me and put an arm around my neck. She studied me thoughtfully, with a faint smile on her face.

"Wha—what's the matter?" I said.

"You really are handsome, Jaime. I don't know if you're aware of that. It's a wonder Simone hasn't made a pass at you."

Not used to this kind of praise, I began to stammer. While I considered myself to be fairly nice looking, I never thought of myself as handsome. Love, or in this case affection, is blind I guess.

"But looks aren't important to me," she said as an afterthought. "It's inside the person that counts. In your case, it's even more beautiful." She kissed me on the cheek, hugged me close, then turned towards the ocean with her arm still around my neck. I had just gathered enough courage to brave her a kiss when she said, "I'm going for a swim." And before I knew it, she was kicking off her shoes. Turning her back to me, she slipped off her dress and let it fall to the ground. The bra and panties came off and I had a brief vision of her naked, loping languidly towards the sea.

I was tempted to follow, but I couldn't bring myself to do it. Having been raised Catholic, I had modesty ingrained in me to the point that I didn't even take showers with other people after gym class. I watched her from a distance pondering on how I should behave when she finally came out completely nude. Should I turn my back while she dressed or should I simply ignore her nudity and talk to her as though she had her clothes on? I snickered. I wouldn't put it past me, I had done sillier things. I could just see myself faking a smile, trying to be cool about it as if such bawdiness happened to me everyday. Then, another thought occurred to me. Maybe I should be straightforward about it and ogle at her. I shook my head. I wished I brought my sunglasses.

When she finally came out, the sun was so low in the horizon I couldn't see her anyway. All I could make out was her dark shadow juxtaposed against the glowing sky. Nevertheless, I keyed in on her feet as she slipped on her dress. Water blotted on the cotton fabric, defining the swell of her breasts and the dark outlines of her pubic hair. Luckily, it was a hot day, and in a few minutes, she would be completely dry.

"It was delicious," she said, balancing herself on my shoulder while she slipped on her shoes. "You should've come in."

I shrugged. "I'm modest. It's this Catholic thing."

"I know."

I raised an eyebrow. "Oh?"

"Tutui is Catholic. Like you, she wouldn't take off her clothes in front of anybody. I find it gracefully innocent."

"Or naively old fashioned," I said disgustedly. It was a trait in me I wanted to shed.

For the second time in an hour, we braved the flight of

steps. But the walk seemed less threatening this time, and I was able to make it to the top without too much of a fuss. By then, it was almost eight.

"Do you know how to get there?" I asked.

She pulled out her ever-present map and began tracing the way. "It's only a few blocks."

Don Pedro's residence was a sprawling estate carved into the cliffs in staggered layers. Nestled under a thick growth of cypress trees, it was white with terracotta roof fenced in by great adobe walls. To get in, one had to come by way of an arched entrance. The green-gated house was open so we entered uninvited.

It was a busy noisy place. Women scurried around the rooms carrying platters of food to the rear patio where a crowd of people, presumably the guests, were having the soiree. The smell of roast meat permeated, and I was at once salivating. Adding to the bustle and confusion were the kids whose energy seemed boundless as they chased each other around a table screaming at the top of their lungs. A woman yelled at them to go outside and they screamed their way past us shooting water pistols at each other. A little girl of about six detached herself from behind her mother's dress. She smiled at us shyly.

"Soy Andrea," she said in a tiny voice.

"Andrea, ven aqui," a woman called out to her. She saw us and smiled. "Hola, you must be Papa's friends." She was about forty, freckled and attractive with a wealth of chestnut hair cascading to her shoulders. "I'm Mildred. Come, come, Papa is waiting at the patio."

She led us into the living room, through a den, down a short flight of steps, and on out to a spacious patio above which was a trellis loaded with flowering boungainvilleas, and from this patio I caught a glimpse of the beautiful Cantabria and its azure water which even at this hour was still dotted with sailboats. The sun was setting, masking the west side of the house with an impasto of pinks and purples.

Don Pedro waved to us. "Jaime, Allison. I'm glad you came," he said effusively. "Come, come. Have a drink of sangria, yes?"

We nodded. The walk up the cliff had dried our throats.

"This is beautiful," Allison said as she gazed out into the bay. Somewhere in the house, a guitar resonated.

I took a sip of the drink. Sweet, tangy with a little bite to it. I twirled it around and saw a slice of orange peel floating in the eddy. "What's in it?" I asked.

"Wine, fruits, juices. La typica bebida Vasca," Don Pedro bragged. One thing I could say about the Basques, they claimed heritage to anything and everything even when it originated from somewhere else.

In all, there must have been thirty guests who attended the party, most of them close relatives of the Guidote clan. To fit everyone together, they joined five substantial wooden tables into one long counter, and I say substantial because their legs were fashioned with weathered oak logs thicker than my thighs, and their flat surfaces, slabs of wood heftier than a medical encyclopedia, and it was only with the aid of an embroidered white linen that Mildred was able to transform them into something halfway gracious.

"But where did you get these tables?" Allison asked.

"Family heirloom," Don Pedro said. "Dates back to the time of the Moors. You can't destroy them." To prove a point, he banged a fist into it, rattling the silverware.

"Papa, be careful," Mildred protested.

Don Pedro motioned to us. "Here, sit beside my nephew Ignacio. He's an artist. You'll find him interesting company."

As the family patriarch, Don Pedro took the head of the table. "And my dear Allison, you can sit on the other side of me and keep this poor old man company."

"You are hogging our guests, Papa," Mildred admonished as she took a seat beside Allison. They served the food on colorful ceramic plates and lined them along the center of the table for easy access to the guests. For appetizers, we had spiced crablegs simmered in garlic tomato sauce and an octopus dish marinaded in oil and vinegar. The crablegs were sumptuous but the octopus I could do without, it was no more pleasurable eating it than a saucerful of rubber bands dipped in Italian dressing. The paella came next, a saffroned rice dish filled with shrimp, crawfish, chicken, and clams which once again Don Pedro claimed had originated from the Basques, and I must confess that having sampled perfect renditions of the dish in Manila and in Bilbao, this one stood out as the best. Its seafood ingredients, I was told, had just been fished out of the Cantabria not more than a few hours ago.

This was accompanied by a serving of blood sausage; medallions of purple meat still smoking from the grill. To my amusement, Allison attacked them with gusto and of her, I must say this: she was probably the only American I knew that would eat just about anything you set in front of her, even though I was later to discover in Andalusia that she also had her limits.

When we got to the rotiserried suckling pigs, Don Pedro did

the honors. With exaggerated flare, he stood up from his seat and draped a white napkin on his forearm. With his free hand, he picked up a clean saucer from the table, and without warning, threw it up in the air, causing Allison to jump up in surprise. The saucer twirled and turned, reaching its peak ascent before falling in a fast spin. Don Pedro reached out, plucking the spinning disc in mid-air, and in one fluid motion, began chopping the piglet into neat thin slices so perfect it could have been chopped by a cleaver. Everyone applauded in glee. All in all, Don Pedro used the saucer on three piglets, leaving the ceramic plate as intact as when he first picked it up. When he finished the last slice, he bowed his head with flourish and tossed the saucer like a frisbee towards the Cantabria. We watched it sail across the patio and disappear over the cliff.

With the ceremony over, everyone dug in. Ignacio, I learned, was both an artist and a musician, and he used his talent interchangeably both as a member of the Bilbao Symphony and a locally renowned painter. He was blond, an unusual trait for a Basque. Paint seemed to have permanently etched itself into the grooves of his forefingers, and as I was talking to him, I noticed that there was a streak of it on his hair and on one cheek prompting me to believe that he must have just pitched his paint brush into a container of turpentine before heading to the party. He alluded to being commissioned by the mayor to renovate the old cathedral in Casco Viejo by painting murals on its ceiling, not unlike Michelangelo's project at Sistine Chapel. In fact, now that he mentioned it, I might have spotted him there when I visited the cathedral, for there were men working on the scaffolding that day.

Throughout dinner, Ignacio stole glances across the table at Mildred who was sitting next to her husband Luis, and I had a distinct feeling that something was going on between them. Out of curiosity, my eyes sought out Mildred's daughter Andrea and confirmed to my satisfaction that she indeed had blond hair, much like Ignacio. While it didn't prove anything, it helped keep my interest at a peak.

Don Pedro speared a chunk of suckling pig and brought it to his mouth. "So, what brought you two lovers to Bilbao?" he asked between swallows. It was an apt question, since no one in his right mind would choose Bilbao as a stopping point for a vacation unless one were into cranes and shipyards.

"We're exchange interns," Allison said. "We're here to pretend to work while waiting for real work."

Don Pedro chuckled. "And I suppose you're also here pretending to be novios." Novios meant boyfriend and girlfriend in Spanish.

Allison blushed.

"But never fear, my young ones. That's the beauty of love. It has to have a certain degree of mystery about it. It is what fascinates the heart."

I suddenly realized that this old man had an uncanny sense of feeling out your psyche. He had us pegged right down to our awkwardness with each other. Anyway, he was right. I wouldn't want to know all there was to know about Allison in one helping. I wanted it divvied out in smidgens and served in a dainty crystal platter so I could savor every bit of detail about her. As I listened to Don Pedro's philosophical reflections, I thought that here was a man who was getting up there in years but had such a colorful outlook on life that he would probably remain young to the day he died.

"And you know what else, my dear ones? If the two of you are as in love as I am seeing you now, nothing will ever stand between you, be it your race, your upbringing, or another man. Nada," he said confidently.

I felt Allison's gaze from across the table. A rosy hue had crept up to her cheeks. Our eyes locked and a current passed between us. It was hard to describe the feeling, but it was during that muted exchange that we first acknowledged our love; the desire to share each other's world, and understand it. Don Pedro saw our gaze. "Ah, how wonderful it is to be in love," he said theatrically, putting his hands to his chest. "But let us not forget that there are other guests at the table and poor Don Pedro is feeling neglected."

Everyone laughed. I could tell Allison was quite taken by Don Pedro. As I was. He was the kind of man one would be proud to have as a father.

The dinner was capped with brandies and puros, thick cigars from the tobacco plantations of Andalusia, and it was at this time that the women began gathering the plates. The men moved the tables to one side, clearing a space for a dance floor.

Ignacio, who had brought his guitar, pulled it out of a leather case and started tuning the chords. A turn of the peg here, a careful twist there, then he began strumming a tango Espanol. His cousin Andres took up a violin and joined him.

One by one, the men and women paired off for this sultry and passionate dance. We watched them from the sidelines, unable to believe the fortuitous events that had transformed the night into a magical experience. What started out as a simple encounter in Bilbao turned into a romantic interlude at Algorda.

Later, when Ignacio strummed a Spanish waltz, Don Pedro pranced over to us. "Allison, would you do the honor of dancing with me?" She smiled at him and extended her arms. I had seen her in action in Cachondo so I knew she could dance, but with a good lead, she was even better.

They twirled on the dance floor like two professional dancers. Waltz was a dance of culture and Don Pedro obviously knew the moves. He did the butterfly and the shadow steps, but always, Allison was able to follow his lead. She pirouetted when she should and twinkled when prompted, and when the tune ended and everyone clapped their hands, Don Pedro made a gallant bow to Allison's gracious curtsy. At that moment, my love for her was so intense I found myself gasping for breath.

Don Pedro brought her to my side. "I was merely borrowing her, chaval." He winked, lowering his voice. "Now she is all yours." He trotted over to another lady and began dancing with her.

Shoulder to shoulder, we stood there in silence, relishing the magic of the moment. The sun had set and in its place rose a glowing moon. Stars dusted the velvet darkness like a million glittering confetti. I gazed at Allison. One side of her face was bathed in moonlight. She smiled up at me. It was a smile of serenity, of happiness, and when Ignacio strummed a slow ballad and his clear wailing voice filled the air, I felt her draw closer.

"Dance with me, Jaime," she whispered.

I nodded speechless. For the first time in my life, I was

truly in love. Taking her hand, I led her to the dance floor. My legs felt like rubber and I could feel my heart floating in my head. And as I took her in my arms and her head settled on my shoulder, we began to sway; slowly, languidly, like a drifting wave. We were lost in our own world. I loved the way she stroked my hair, the way she snuggled close to me, I loved the soothing warmth of her body, the softness of her skin. Minutes ticked and they seemed like hours. And when she whispered something in my ear that I couldn't quite catch, I leaned closer only to hear the magic words. "Kiss me," she breathed. Tilting her chin up, I gazed into her eyes, seeing for the first time the depth of her love. I kissed her tenderly. I felt the softness of her lips, the passion of her embrace. My heart soared to dizzying heights.

When she broke off the kiss, she hugged me tightly. "Oh God, I've never felt this way before," she whispered.

I wanted to say something but was too overcome with emotion to come up with the right words. And so I simply drew her closer and made a silent wish that the night would never end.

I felt a tap on my shoulders. I turned and saw Don Pedro standing next to us.

"Sorry to interrupt your bliss, my dear ones, but it is time for the fiesta," he said. The music had stopped and we were the only ones left on the dance floor. Allison disengaged herself from me. Face flushed, she ran a hand through her hair.

"I see you two have finally found each other," Don Pedro said. "I am happy for you."

When everyone had assembled in the living room, Don

Pedro said, "Now, let's not get separated. Mildred, make sure the children are accompanied." He slipped the bota bag over his shoulders and beckoned us to follow.

We stepped out of the gate and were immediately swallowed by the crowd. To my astonishment, the town which not more than a few hours ago was a peaceful enclave, had metamorphosed into a nocturnal circus. The atmosphere was electric as dancing revelers howled in glee.

We followed the surging crowd, making an effort not to lose each other in the chaos. Don Pedro took Allison's hand and she took mine and we all danced uphill weaving our way towards the plaza, singing, "O Kaiku, que to eres el amo..." a Basque song I had heard in the various fiestas of Bilbao. It was a time to drink, a time to celebrate, a time to lose oneself to childish merriment.

Every bar in town had opened its doors. They overflowed with people. Everywhere I turned I saw barbecue grills billowing thick clouds of smoke into the night. We reached the plaza where earlier in the day Don Pedro had recounted the history of Algorda, and here in this town square, we saw hordes of wild-eyed celebrants, much more in numbers than in any other part of town, for this appeared to be the focal point of the celebration. The luminous lights that Don Pedro and his crew had so meticulously strung now glowed in a profusion of rainbow hues. On a stage gazebo in one corner of the square, a six-man band in traditional fiesta costume played a catchy version of accordion folk music. Even the black-hatted Guardia Civil were out in force, cradling their gleaming machine pistols, sternly watching the crowd. But people were enjoying themselves too much to even bother with them.

With glazed eyes, I took in the excitement, feeling an overpowering rush surging through my veins. In the vicinity of the stage, people had formed a circle to dance the traditional Basque solta, an acrobatic dance that involved kicking your feet in the air and jumping as high as you can. It required the strength and dexterity of someone in good shape, for not only did you have to make a number of successive leaps, you also had to do it while holding the hands of dancers on either side of you. Allison and I watched them entranced. Up, down, up, down, they went, kicking and shouting as they did so. "Aupa! Venga mas fuerte!" Their jumps rose higher and their kicking intensified until that final leap when they somersaulted in midair and landed on their feet in unison.

As the dancers left the floor clapping each other on the back, the band began to play the waltz. Everyone paired up, even the little girls. I took Allison's hand and led her to the dance floor and while I couldn't execute Don Pedro's fancy moves, I knew enough to hold my own. It was five minutes of fantasia during which we giggled and twirled like two little kids.

Don Pedro beckoned to us afterwards. "Follow me," he said, leading us towards the center of the plaza where they had just built a roaring bonfire. People were gathered around it as young men in Basque costumes hurtled themselves across the blaze to their cheering friends on other side.

"Let me do it, let me do it," Don Pedro exclaimed.

"Por favor, Papa. No, it's too dangerous," Mildred protested. The fire had grown bigger. But if Don Pedro heard her, he gave no indication. With an air of bravado, he took a step back, one leg bent like a speed skater, and without further ado, began a mad sprint towards the fire. Allison's hand tightened against mine. For an old man, he was going quite fast, but I feared not fast enough for a solid leap. He quickly closed the gap and for an instant, I wondered if he could even make it across.

Two feet from the fire, he took one last stride and hurtled himself in the air. He punched through the flames with his arms doing cartwheels, and strangely enough, landed safely on the other side. People clapped in glee.

Ignacio followed him across, then Roberto, then Andres, and finally, Mildred's husband Luis. Mildred's frown deepened.

"Jaime! Jaime Aragon! Te toca! It's your turn!" Don Pedro called out from across the bonfire. He waved his arm frantically.

"Don't do it, Jaime," Allison said. Her lips had paled as she gaped at the fire which had now blossomed into a raging inferno. Flames licked skyward, sending millions of orange sparks into the darkness. I felt its intense heat on my face. But by then, the adrenaline was flowing.

They began to chant, "Jai-me, Jai-me, Jai-me!" I found myself dashing towards the fire, timing my steps to get the best momentum possible. Somehow, I must clear the surging flames and land eight feet on the other side. Anything short would be disastrous.

I counted as I ran: five-six-seven-eight. Three feet from the blaze, I flung myself across. I felt myself soaring, felt the surging heat, the threatening roar. Walls of flames engulfed me. Suddenly, I was stumbling on the other side into the waiting arms of Luis and Ignacio.

Later, when we stopped for a drink in one of the outdoor cafes in the plaza, Allison scolded me. I had never seen her so furious. "That was foolish, Jaime," she fumed. "What if you were hurt? They would have sent you home." Suddenly, I realized the stupidity of my actions. It would have spoiled my plans, put my life in jeopardy. Worse yet, it would have put an end to whatever we had going between us.

"You—you're right, Allison. I'm sorry. I didn't think." I touched her arm. "Will you forgive me?" She shouldered me away.

"Please," I said.

She measured me with her eyes. That cornered look again. What the heck is bothering her? But as quickly as it came, it was gone. "Yes," she said finally. "But don't do it again." She came into my arms. I felt her shiver. "I wouldn't know what to do if something happened to you, Jaime...I simply wouldn't."

Don Pedro came out with a bottle of wine. "Drink up amigos. That was a good leap you just made, Jaime. You are now an honorary Basque." He nodded to Allison. "So, how do you like the Fiesta de Algorda, chiquita?"

"Except for that part about the fire, I love it. It—it's so energetic—so vibrant." I nodded in agreement. There was something about these fiestas that lifted your spirit, and if I were to describe then what Spanish life was like, I would compare it to a fiesta and not be far off. Live for the present and the hell with the consequences.

I glanced at the bonfire, and that was when I spotted Francisco fifty feet away with a gymbag slung over his shoulder. He was with the two men I saw him with at the university. They were walking rapidly towards the center of the square. I glanced at Allison. She was turned the other way. Good, I thought. Nothing to spoil our evening.

"Well, let me make another jump," Don Pedro said.

"Papa," Mildred protested, to no avail. But by then, the fire had died down so she let him go.

When Andres and Mildred's husband Luis trailed after him, Mildred rolled her eyes in disgust. "Such stubborn men," she bristled.

"Yeah, it's this man thing, Mildred," Allison said, looking at me with meaning.

I was about to protest this feminist remark when a powerful explosion rocked the plaza. It was so huge it killed the bonfire and sent debris raining in all directions. Body parts flew. A bloody head landed on the pavement, bounced twice like a soccer ball, and rolled the distance to our table. Allison jerked back from her chair, shrieking at the grotesque face. Mildred and I sat with our mouths open, caught in complete surprise. There was a brief second of inactivity, then anarchy erupted. People started screaming.

Suddenly, the square was filled with the moaning wounded trying to crawl away from the huge hole in the ground. Blood coated the pavement in a gleaming wet film, and as I stood up from my chair after recovering from the initial shock, I realized just how lucky we had been, for not more than a few minutes ago, we were standing in the exact location of the blast. I staggered towards the square, weak-kneed from the carnage. A thin haze of smoke hung over the plaza. It scorched my nose, stung my eyes.

"Don Pedro! Andres! Luis!" I called out, straining my ears for an answering call, knowing there would be none coming. I stepped on a piece of flesh and almost slipped. My stomach fluttered as I steadied myself. Oh God, I thought. The smell of blood swept into my nostrils.

Gingerly, I walked farther into the square, trying not to look at the mindless slaughter. That was when I found Don Pedro among the rubble of brick and wood. His body had been rudely dismembered across the waist. His face was blackened and lacerated. Strangely enough, his bota bag survived the blast, still attached to a dangling shoulder. I became aware of Allison standing next to me. She issued a small cry. I took her in my arms and forced her head to my chest, knowing that somewhere in the rubble were the mangled bodies of Andres and Luis.

The ambulances came, fifteen white vans and fifteen white cars wailing their way through the crowded alleys. Eeeeyo-Eeeeyo-Eeeeyo! their sirens screamed as they barreled into the plaza in a swirl of blue lights, heading straight to the center of the square where the blast had created a gaping excavation. We found ourselves being roughly herded away by the Guardia Civil, who in a matter of minutes had efficiently taken control of the plaza, erecting makeshift barriers around the vicinity of the blast.

We searched for Mildred and her family, but couldn't find them anywhere. Thinking that they might have gone home, we marched back to the house. Only a few of them had made it back, and those that did were dazed and confused. Mildred wasn't among them. Her daughter Andrea had awakened from her sleep and was crying for her mother, and as I stared at her in that living room in the midst of the chaos, I thought to myself that this family, who in a single night had lost at least three of its members, would never be the same again.

Unable to bear their suffering, we walked away from the

house. Oddly enough, I couldn't shed a tear, I couldn't even think. What had begun as a magical night of romance had turned into a gruesome nightmare. And as we wandered our way towards the train station, we encountered people in the same petrified condition. They walked in subdued silence unable to believe that their peaceful little town whose last known carnage was in the hands of the Moors had been forever marred by the violence of modern terrorism.

We followed the crowd down the street, taking a side route to the train station whose platform was packed with people wanting to escape the night's terror. There was an atmosphere of hysteria about the place reminiscent of an impending disaster, except in this case, the disaster had already struck. Allison still hadn't spoken a word, which worried me.

Afraid of losing her in the crowd, I grabbed her hand and fell into line, and it was not long before a loud whistle blasted out of the tunnel.

The train chugged into the terminal and came to a grating stop in front of us, belching smoke from its underbelly. Immediately, the crowd surged forward sweeping us through the double doors all the way into the back of the train, and it was only through luck that we were able to find seats, for the aisle filled up in mere seconds.

When we had settled down and the train was on its way, Allison broke into shivers. Her lips quivered like a child's and her eyes grew round and big. I took her in my arms and hugged her close. It was the best I could do. I was as lost in the tragedy as she was. Don Pedro, while a complete stranger, had sparked something in us. It was he who framed into words our affection for each other and fanned it into a flame with his humorous encouragement. But more distressing to us than his loss was the appalling magnitude of the carnage, for there could easily have been hundreds of people dead and wounded in that plaza. I blocked off the thought. I dared not lose my nerve. Somehow, I must get us home safely.

I became aware of my bloodstained pants and lifted a leg to inspect it. To my alarm, I saw that my one and only decent pair of shoes was ruined, the blood having soaked into the leather turning its surface into a mottled black. I stared at it stupidly as if it was the most important thing in the world. The man in front of me leaned forward. "Are you okay?" he asked.

I nodded mutely. He himself was spattered with blood. I wanted to cry, but it was not a manly thing to do.

☼ 13 The Caravan

It took an excruciating hour to make it to Bilbao. Even though it was only ten o'clock, very few people stood waiting at the station when we got off, raising my concern that perhaps there was a mad bomber on the loose planting explosives in crowded places. Had people been warned to stay away?

I began to fret. I knew I was being overly paranoid, but paranoia had a way of getting out of hand once started.

I steered Allison out of the station, avoiding the crowded avenidas of the city, and after ten minutes of walking during which neither one of us spoke, we finally reached the building. Thank God, I thought, wiping my face with my sleeves. Safe at last.

But anxious as we were to get to our fourth floor apartment, we never quite made it there, for the minute we reached third, we were greeted by a party in full swing with people spilling out of the apartment units all the way to the stairwell.

Everyone was there: Bjorn, Elena, Cliff, Miguel, Simone, Iñaki, Jose Mari, and many others I didn't know or had never met. I looked at them in confusion wondering if I hadn't been privy to something previously planned until it dawned on me that we were supposed to be celebrating the arrival of a new batch of exchange interns. Iñaki waved to us enthusiastically until he noticed the blood on our clothes.

"Por Dios, what happened?" he asked, aghast.

"They bombed Algorda," I said. Everyone gathered around us.

"Bu—but there is a fiesta down there," Iñaki protested. Blood drained from his face.

"I know..."

"I—I have to call my sister," he said. Without another word, he scrambled down the steps heading towards the phone booth on the first floor.

"His sister lives in Algorda," Jose Mari explained.

As I recounted my story to a rapt audience, I saw Elena leading Allison up the steps. She caught my eye and motioned upstairs. I gave her a thankful nod then turned to answer a few more questions. Suddenly, I was tired. My eyelids felt like bags of concrete. "Listen guys. I can't talk anymore. I think I'm turning in."

Exhausted, I climbed up the steps to our apartment and found Elena closing the door to her bedroom.

"Esta dormiendo," she said. "She's asleep. I gave her some tranquilizers."

"Thanks," I said wearily. I wouldn't have been able to take care of her much longer. And as if to confirm this point, I began to tremble. I had held it for two hours and now I couldn't stop. I leaned against the wall and closed my eyes. My teeth chattered.

Elena took me in her arms. "It's all right, querido, it's all right." She stroked my hair.

"It—it was horrible, Elena. All those dead people..."

"Shhh, querido. I know, but you must not think about it. Try to forget." She took something from her shirt pocket and pressed it into my hand. It was a couple of blue pills.

"Take it. It will help you fall asleep." She kissed me on the cheek. "Are you going to be all right here?"

I sighed. "Yeah, I'll be alright."

Thanking her, I trudged into the bedroom. I peeled off my bloody clothes and wrapped them in Bjorn's copy of El Pais so I wouldn't stain the Señora's furniture. Slipping into my pajamas, I crawled into bed, hugging myself under the blanket.

Even in exhaustion, sleep eluded me. My mind kept drifting back to the plaza: the explosion, the rolling head, the wet gleaming film on the pavement. I stifled a cry, fought off the images. Mercifully, the pills took their toll and I was swallowed up by sleep, and it was not long before I found myself in a delirium. Allison...Don Pedro...me...dancing in the plaza. We were laughing playfully, making faces at each other like three little kids. Slowly, they detached themselves from me. They waltzed away, around and around the plaza, twirling, turning, swaying closer to the bonfire. Stop! I cried out in alarm. Don't!

I was answered by a muted silence.

Desperately, I called out to them again and this time, they turned. Come back! I yelled. Come back! There's a bomb! But the more I yelled, the less they seemed to comprehend. To my horror, they resumed dancing. Each step they made brought them closer to the fire. Then I saw a face, a familiar face, and I was instantly overcome by fear. Get away from them, I screamed at the man. Get away! But the man sneered at me; mocking me, taunting me, and as if to confirm my worst fears, he pulled out a large bomb from his gymbag which he derisively waved. Then, with a final laughter, he slipped the black box into Allison's tote bag.

Allison! Allison! Your purse! There's a bomb! I cried out in despair. Suddenly, my pleadings were interrupted by a huge explosion. Two heads rocketed out of the blast, arced its way across the black sky, and landed on the pavement. They bounced and rolled, coming to a stop in front of me.

I gasped in horror as I recognized Allison and Don Pedro's lacerated heads. Their eyes popped open and stared at me accusingly. *Why didn't you tell us, Jaime, they uttered in unison. Why?*

I sat up with a moan. Sweat poured down my face. I cast a wild glance around the room and saw Bjorn fast asleep on the other bed. Only a dream, I thought in relief. Then I remembered Algorda and was overtaken by sudden shudders. With a cry, I staggered out of bed and stumbled my way into the kitchen. Dousing myself with water at the sink, I glanced out the window. Sun filtered through the warped pane making a prism on my shirt. Morning, I breathed thankfully.

Pulling away, I shook my head, trying to clear the fog. A veil seemed to have wrapped itself around my brain. My lips trembled. A tic quivered on my cheekbone. *You can't let her see you like this.*

Staggering into the bedroom, I slipped into my jogging

pants. I thought of writing her a note, but something held me back. It was a strange feeling. I simply had to get away.

Guiltily, I tiptoed out the door, glided down the stairs, and saw myself streaking along the boulevard towards the river. I jogged for miles, from the foot of the Deusto Bridge to the shipyards of Zarzuela, I raced by the factory where I worked, cantered past the building Allison worked and still I pushed on. I could hear my labored gasps as I trotted up one hill and down another. I jogged for two hours, never stopping, never taking a break, pushing myself, punishing, until in the end, I couldn't run anymore.

At an isolated country road that forked towards Burgos, I stopped at a grassy knoll. Around me stood a grove of oak trees. My chest heaved and I stood gasping for air. Leaning against a tree trunk, I gazed out into the city. I could see Bilbao in the distance with its great twisting river and sprawl of edifices. In the few months I had been living there, it had grown on me by leaps and bounds. I knew somewhere out there were my friends, my roommates...and my new found love, Allison.

With trembling legs, I sat down on the grass and closed my eyes in exhaustion. I thought about Algorda and felt a piercing ache spiking up my chest. My eyes burned. The diary, Jaime. Do it. It will help ease your pain. Reluctantly, I pulled out a notepad from my back pocket. I propped it on my lap.

I wrote for three hours jotting down everything that came to mind; my loves, my fears, my sufferings. But most of all, I wrote about Allison; she was foremost in my mind. Words flowed out of my fingers like magic, evoking in me emotions I never thought I had such that in some instances, I found myself welling up in tears. My love for Allison was so great I knew I was in danger of being swept away. But foolish as it might seem, I could no longer hold it back even if I wanted to. I had gotten to the fifth page when out of the corner of my eye, I saw movement coming in from the west.

I turned cautiously. This was supposed to be an untraveled spot. To my astonishment, I saw a long caravan of horse-drawn wagons weaving its way down the road. There must have been twenty of them led by three battered cars whose rear bumpers were burdened by three equally battered trailers. Behind them, scattered around the plains roamed a herd of horses.

The cars whipped by and proceeded to a patch of gravel a few meters away. Dust billowed out of their tires. The lead wagon, a red cart with a striped canvas top halted in front of me, and I couldn't help but notice that it was bigger than the rest and the only striped one in the all white procession. A man of about fifty sat on the driver's seat, regarding me contemplatively.

My creative energy interrupted, I looked at him in irritation. I wondered what in the world such a man would want from me until I realized that I might not be the one he wanted but the spot I was sitting on. After all, it was 96 degrees in the shade, and I was hogging the part of the hill that had ample trees.

A young woman rode up on a horse, face glowing with vitality. She pranced the skittish animal this way and that and I swiftly recognized her as the Gypsy girl to whom I had given the fifty-peseta coin that fateful night at Cachondo, the one who had cried at the side of the fallen Gypsy. She was wearing the same sleeveless blouse, the same red skirt, the same green espadrilles, but where there used to be a gold necklace around her neck were now strands of beads. In the daylight, she was even prettier than I remembered. The sun brought out her uniquely exotic features from the thick sun-bleached hair and rich eyebrows to the wide mouth with a trace of the pout. Her tan was almost gold as if she had spent an inordinate amount of time on the beaches of St. Tropez.

"We need a place to rest," she declared in accented English, then did a double take when she recognized me.

"You!" she exclaimed.

I gave her a lopsided smile, then remembered the dead Gypsy. I turned serious. "I'm sorry about your friend. I tried..."

"No-no, do not apologize. He lived. You saved his life."

I couldn't believe my ears. Alive! After Algorda, I needed the good news.

"My brother is weak but he is alive," she explained. "When you pushed him out of the way, the knife missed his heart. But it grazed his lung. That's why all that blood was coming out of his mouth. But the doctors were able to stop the bleeding. In fact, he's out there now with the horses."

"But it had only been three weeks."

"I know, and he can't ride for too long. He's just helping round up the horses."

She walked back to the man on the striped wagon and spoke to him in rapid Spanish. The man nodded. He bellowed an order to the rest of the caravan. Instantly, everyone was scrambling around. They skipped off the wagons and set up camp with amazing speed, and of them, I could say this: they were probably the most efficient group of people I had ever seen at least in the art of setting up camp, for in less than ten minutes, they had erected the tents, spread the blankets on the ground, stoked the fires, and had kettles going. At first, no one spoke to me engrossed as they were with the chores of camp, but when the activity had settled down, the girl came back with her saddle. She sat down next to me by the fire.

"I'm Arianna. I am sorry for barging into you like this," she said in English.

"No problem. I was just resting." I smiled. "I'm Jaime, by the way. Jaime Aragon."

She looked at me reflectively, her gaze like twin daggers aimed at my eyes. I began to wonder if I had done anything that might have upset her. "You're not Spanish," she said. "Morrocan?"

"Far East. Manila," I said.

Her question didn't surprise me. In the six weeks I had been here, I had been mistaken for a Venezuelan, an Argentinean, a Pakistani, a Chinese, a Tahitian, an African, and a vagabond Gypsy. It was perhaps the trait about me that incited the most curiosity since all my relationships, platonic or otherwise, started out with this overriding question about my origins. Even Allison, who claimed not to take physical attributes into consideration when dating men, admitted to it.

I nodded to the wagons. "Where are you heading?"

"South. To Andalusia." She ran her tapered fingers through her hair. "We live in Les Saintes Maries de la Mer in Southern France but we travel to Spain every summer for the carnivals and horse fairs."

"But there were more of you in Cachondo," I said.

"That is true. It's because we joined up with the

Manouches and Sintis who are carnival performers from Germany. They're heading to Castille to put on carnival shows at various town fiestas."

"What's in Andalusia?"

"You've never been?"

"No."

"Well, family for one thing. There is a big colony of Gypsies in Salamanca, Triana, and in Zoco. We usually swing west first then east. But for extranjeros, there are lots to see. Bullfights, flamenco dances, ferias. There are more things going on there that are typically Spanish than here. Of course, it is also much poorer."

I nodded. I had never heard or seen a bullfight in all these months I had been living in Bilbao, with the possible exception of the Fiesta de San Fermines at Pamplona. I asked Mr. Saturnino about this once and he told me that Bilbainos didn't like bullfights. 'They're not a Basque tradition,' he said. 'Jai-alai and wood chopping yes, but not bullfights.'

"I may visit the south some day," I said dreamily. My eyes drifted around the camp and took in the shipshape condition of their wagons, the fine horses they brought along on the pilgrimage and thought, these people are not poor at all, at least not the way they made them out to be in books. In fact, dust of travel aside, they were a fairly well-groomed lot. Their clothes were not new, but they were clean and in good condition. She must have read my mind, because she said, "Our tribe has been lucky. We had five good years of foaling and we were able to buy a small ranch in the South of France. But there are Gypsies who are so poor they had to steal from other people to put bread in their mouths."

"I thought all Gypsies stole," I said, and quickly regretted the slip. She took on a hurt look. "I'm sorry, I didn't mean that. It's just that I heard—I mean people have told me..." I was grasping at straws.

"You don't have to explain, Jaime. In a sense, we did it to ourselves. We had been stealing for centuries and we still do. It's part of our make up. Sometimes I think we got it from the Moors."

"Did you ever?"

She looked at me as though I were crazy. "Of course. I wouldn't be a true Gypsy if I didn't. But that was a long time ago."

I noticed that she spoke English in concise sentences, and thought that this girl was not some barefooted nomad from the dry creeks of Extremedura but rather an educated one with a lot of practical savvy—she seemed to be respected by the older members of the tribe. "Where did you learn English?"

"In Liverpool. When I was seven, my father sent me to live with my aunt. There's a big Gypsy settlement there. I went to an English school for a couple of years."

I studied the round mole on the right side of her chin just below the lower lip. In Manila, it was supposed to be the mark of chattiness. I wondered what it meant to the Gypsies. "What does the mole mean?"

"It means I'm a gossiper." She laughed the answer. "I'm supposed to not be able to hold a secret."

"Hey, that's the same belief we have in Manila."

Her eyes widened as she squinted at something behind me. "Montalvo is coming," she said.

At a distant hill, a rider was making his way down the

slope. He maneuvered his spotted horse around a boulder then trotted it down the trail towards camp. He dismounted in front of us.

The man was a male version of Arianna except much taller and with fiercer countenance. He was gaunt, but healthy in color.

"This is the man that saved you, Montalvo," Arianna said. "His name is Jaime."

His eyes widened. "Por dios. I've been looking all over for you," he said. "I even took a special trip to Baracaldo to see the Italian brothers. They didn't know where you live."

I took his offered hand. "It's nothing, really. I just reacted, that's all. I didn't even think."

"That doesn't change the fact that you saved my life, amigo," he said. "Tell me, how can I ever repay you?"

I waved it off. "Really, don't worry about it. No te preoccupes."

"My friend. There's one thing you have to know about Gypsies. Steal we may but we settle our debts."

I mulled over what he said and came up with a compromise that might work for him. In fact, it was a darned exciting one. My heart raced just thinking about it. "Tell you what. Arianna was just telling me about Zoco. Why don't I keep the marker and when I hitch a ride there later this summer, then we can settle."

Someone started banging on a frying pan. I turned towards the noise.

"Lunch time," Arianna said.

They brought out the plates and began stroking the kettles. Arianna insisted that I stay and before I could respond, wisely pushed a bowl into my hand. "Come," she said. "Let's get something to eat."

It was a simple meal: a steaming bowl of garbanzo soup with large chunks of linguisa and cabbage. Lots of fried garlic. Not having had anything to eat since my dinner at Don Pedro's house the night before, I wolfed down the food.

The grizzled old man on the wagon which I surmised was Arianna's father joined us in the circle. He began talking to me in heavily-accented Spanish quite unlike any I had ever heard. His was more guttural, primitive. I later learned from Arianna that he was the Vovoide of the tribe or the chieftain. I noticed the gun tucked beneath the folds of his vest but I didn't let it bother me. I felt safe with them.

He asked me the same questions Arianna did; where I was from, what I was doing here, how long I was staying, and if I planned to visit the south. He thanked me for saving his son's life and once again pressed me to accept payment which I politely declined.

Sensing my obvious discomfort about the subject, Arianna steered the conversation to the coming horse fair at Zoco to which everyone responded with great enthusiasm, and even though a lot of the gibber was Gypsy 'horse-speak,' I skimmed enough of the exchange to learn that Zoco was the final destination of the pilgrimage. From afar, someone stroked a guitar and wailed a Gypsy song. It was poignant, filled with emotion, I listened to it entranced.

"Do you like it?" Arianna asked. She moved closer.

"Yes. It's beautiful. What is it?"

"It's a Gypsy song about a man who fell in love with a woman from another tribe," Arianna said. "But they were so different from each other that their love was doomed from the start. You see, he is a Gitano from Andalusia and she is a Sinti from Germany. A Gypsy is forbidden to marry outside his tribe. The song ends with the two lovers ultimately breaking up. The tribe's pressure forced him to shy away from the woman. It so broke his heart that he left his tribe to wander on his own, thinking that maybe he could find another woman. Except that kind of opportunity only comes once in a lifetime. In the end, he died of a broken heart." She looked at me. "Sad, isn't it?"

I nodded. A dull ache squeezed at my chest. I saw her watching me and averted my eyes.

She touched my arm. "You are running away from someone, aren't you?"

I bowed my head. Running away. A good way to put it.

"Your girlfriend?"

"I don't know what we are," I said. "All I know is that we care for each other."

"Don't be like that man in the song, Jaime. Love can be painful. Frightening too sometimes. But in the end, it is always worth it."

I glanced at her and thought that here was a girl any man would be lucky to have. There was a depth to her, much like Allison when she philosophized about life.

I stayed with them until sunset, listening to stories about carnivals and pilgrimages and horse fairs and in those few short hours, I learned more about the gypsy life than I would ever learn in a book. I tried to imagine what it would be like traveling every single day without any real destination in mind. I wondered if that's how life is. Some meaningless journey. I thought of Allison and shook my head. Life with her would never be meaningless.

I glanced at my watch. Six o'clock. If I were to make it back before dark, I had better get started.

After thanking my hosts for their hospitality, I started down the trail towards Bilbao. I followed the winding road, passing the makeshift corrals they had erected for the night, and as I turned towards the path that would take me over the hill to Zarzuela, I saw a man on a horse watching me from under the trees. He was a handsome man with a black sombrero and a black embroidered waist coat. Too dressed up to be a mere herdsman. I felt the strength of his gaze, and for no apparent reason, became apprehensive. Allison, I thought, and felt fear crawling in my stomach.

I arrived at about eight and found them at the El Caracol Bar. Bjorn and Elena were at the pinball machine. The others were spread out at the tables having the usual peanuts and carinena wine. Cigarette butts littered their feet. My eyes sought out Allison but didn't find her anywhere.

Elena took me aside. Her face was livid. "Dammit Jaime. How could you leave her like that? She was looking all over for you."

I shook my head. I didn't know. "Wh—where is she?"

"She went out looking for Francisco."

"Francisco," I muttered. Something kicked me in the gut.

"I have to go," I said suddenly. With a sourness rising up in my throat, I raced across Plaza San Pedro. Urgency clouded my vision. I didn't know what had gotten into me, only that Allison might be in some kind of danger.

I darted towards the university, and cut across the lawn

towards the side entrance of the dormitory where I spotted Francisco and his friends one night. Someone was smoking outside. For a moment, I thought it was the same man, until I drew closer and saw that he was clean cut. Not the long-haired stocky man under the trees that night.

I approached. "Francisco Marbella—su habitacion. Donde esta," I demanded in a rush of breath.

The man gave a start, intimidated by my sudden appearance. "Ah—numero doce," he replied.

Shouldering past him, I entered the building and stalked down the hallway. Florescent lights blinked overhead. Number 12 was at the end of the hall next to the Coke machines.

I banged on the door. "Francisco! Are you in there?"

Nothing.

I banged again, looking around wildly.

Stepping outside, I circled the building, slid past a row of bushes and found the back window under the wings of an oak tree. I peered inside. Pitch black. A digital clock glowed in the dark. She's not here, I thought. Instinctively, my eyes turned towards our apartment building which was visible from this vantage point. A light was on. Had it been there before?

◆◆◆

I scrambled up the flight of stairs, reached the fourth floor landing, and found the apartment door ajar. Except for the crack of light under Allison's door, the hallway was completely dark.

I found her in the bedroom lying face down on the bed. She was crying silently. She made no sound; just a shaking of the shoulders. I suddenly felt rotten. How could I have abandoned her? I didn't even leave a note.

Sitting down on the bed, I placed a hand on her shoulder. "I'm sorry I left. It was an insensitive thing to do."

Her shoulders stiffened, but she didn't say anything.

I pulled my hand away. "I don't know what came over me, Allison. It's just that felt I needed to get away—clear my head."

Again silence.

"I want you to know that I thought about you all day."

No response.

"Did you find him?" I asked.

She shook her head. For some reason, I knew she wouldn't.

I sighed. "Do you love him, Allison?"

Again, no answer.

She's shutting me out, I thought. I gazed at her for a moment, uncertain what to do next. I had an urge to grab her, talk some sense into her. But I knew it would only make it worse.

"Do you want me to leave?"

She nodded on the pillow. Wearily, I stood up. I badly needed a drink. At this point, I didn't think we could ever overcome Algorda. We would share it for the rest of our lives, for better or for worse, and every time she looked at me from now on, she would see that big blast at the plaza, the macabre head bouncing towards her, and Don Pedro's mangled body with the bota bag still attached to him.

I took Bjorn's bottle of aquavit from the kitchen counter and poured myself a drink. I took it in one gulp and poured myself another. The heat of the alcohol seared into my belly.

But it didn't deaden the pain. I began to question fate. Why was it that each time I found a woman to love, something always came along to ruin it? I felt victimized. It seemed so unfair.

Hugging the bottle, I trudged to my bedroom and lay down on the bed. Tears leaked out of my eyes. It wasn't supposed to be like this. I was only twenty-three. At home, I had the support of my friends, my family, and even though that support often consisted of intangible reassurances, at least I had someone to lean on, carry me through the ordeal. Here, I was on my own, floundering around like a drowning man. And as if it were not enough, I now had Allison to worry about because the reality was, she had become my responsibility, just as I had become hers. The night she scolded me when I took that foolish leap across the bonfire was a glaring testimony to that.

I stifled a yawn. My eyelids drooped. I found myself drifting off to sleep. Images surfaced. Jumbled like a scrap book. There was Allison's face...the two of us at the bus stop...the Bertendon Gardens. Marina's face came and went. Allison again. The next thing I remember, I was being shaken awake.

"Jaime," Bjorn said. "The guys are thinking of going to the beach today."

I blinked wide. The sun glared at me through the open window. My eyes darted towards Allison's room.

"She's coming," he said. He picked up his Viking comic books and stuffed them in a backpack.

"Okay, give me a minute to get ready. What time is it anyway?"

"Ten."

I shot up in bed. "God, I've overslept."

"Hey, take it easy. We'll wait for you."

I took my clothes and hurried into the bathroom.

☼ 14 Falling Star

I ran into Allison in the kitchen. Strangely enough, she seemed to have recovered.

"Hi Jaime," she said. She dried the cereal bowl with a dishrag and replaced it in the cupboard.

"Hi Allison."

"I'm sorry about last night. I—I was just so upset by what happened."

I touched her arm. "You don't have to explain. I felt the same way. That's why I left. I didn't know how to face you."

She looked away. "I understand."

Did she? She seemed so distant. I struggled for the right words to say. "About Algorda—is it real—I mean—about us?"

She gazed up at me; nodded. But there was a sullen look on her face. "Yes, it's real, Jaime. I just don't know if it's the right thing to do."

"Why not?" I asked gently. But she only shrugged. And so

she wouldn't have to explain herself, she came into my arms and buried her face in my neck.

As we waited for everyone to collect their things, we slipped downstairs so we could be alone. We stood under the shade of a myrtle tree watching the Sunday churchgoers at Plaza San Pedro. We held hands, but she avoided any further talk of our relationship or what happened in Algorda. Maybe it was the wrong thing to do, a psychiatrist would surely have recommended the opposite. And because I felt unfairly shut out, I took her in my arms and roughly kissed her. It was not a sweet kiss, but she melted in my arms and responded to it with passion. Her hands grasped at my hair as she mashed her lips into mine. Her tongue lashed at me urgently, her teeth biting at my lower lip and it was at that moment that I felt her agitation.

When she broke it off, she was panting heavily. For a brief second, she had that look of anger and arousal on her face. But it quickly disappeared. She put her head on my chest, shivering. "I love you, Jaime. I love you so much it frightens me sometimes."

At last, I thought ecstatically. An admission of love. After months of dreaming and hoping and living through all sorts of heartache, I had finally won her over. But even as I celebrated this sweet victory, I couldn't help but feel a certain amount of anxiety. Maybe I felt vulnerable; I had opened myself up too much. Maybe I wanted to avoid a repeat of Algorda; an evening of bliss shattered by unexpected tragedy. Whatever it was, the feeling followed me through the walk to the ferry terminal.

I remembered the day clearly. It was a beautiful day. Lots

of chirping birds and sparkling sunshine. The others had joined us with their towels and totebags and straw picnic baskets. Allison and I were up in front with Bjorn and Elena slightly behind us busy rubbing suntan lotion on their faces. On our left was the university campus.

A group of summer students had just emerged from the dorm, strutting on the grass lawn towards the gate. There were three of them, and I remembered squinting in the sun because I thought they looked familiar. As they drew nearer, I recognized Francisco and his two friends.

I was swiftly overcome by a deep foreboding. My eyes darted towards Allison whose steps had now quickened. Her eyes got rounder, and I knew she was about to call out to him. Suddenly, from along the avenida came a swarm of Seats with blue lights flashing. There must have been eight of them, each forbiddingly quiet moving at a fast speed towards the university.

The trio who had just reached the gate, saw the speeding caravan and froze. They shouted something to each other and started running in the opposite direction.

There was a screech of tires as the police reached the gate. Men spilled out of cars.

I saw Francisco turn, his arm whipping out. His friends followed suit. Pop! Pop! Pop! Puffs of smoke rose out of their hands. The police lifted their rifles and Allison gave an anguished cry. "Noooo!" she wailed, and started running down the hill.

I took off after her, grabbing her from behind just as a series of pops broke the stillness. Francisco pitched backwards. Blots of red appeared on his shirtfront.

The police fired unremittingly, jerking the trio this way and that like ragdolls. By the time they stopped shooting, Francisco and his friends lay sprawled on the ground.

Allison sobbed uncontrollably. She tried to shake me off but I tightened my grip. Afraid the Guardia Civil would see us, I dragged her behind a tree and pulled her to my chest. She convulsed in my arms, her body racked by agonized sobs. Her suffering so angered me that I stared up in the heavens and cursed at God for His unending cruelty. What did she do to deserve this? I screamed in my mind. Wasn't Algorda enough?

When we took her home a few minutes later, she was a whimpering mess. She couldn't walk, let alone take care of herself. Tucking her into bed, we forced a couple of pills into her mouth. She moaned for a few minutes but was eventually swallowed up by sleep.

I glanced at Elena who was gazing down at Allison, stroking her hair. She was like a mother caring for a sick child. Her lower lip pushed out and for a second, I thought she was going to burst out crying. Hoping to avoid another weeping woman in my hands, I quietly led her and Bjorn to the door.

"Go ahead to the beach, Elena. I'll take care of her."

Elena hesitated.

"Please," I said. I glanced back towards the bed, knowing no amount of company would help Allison that day. She had as much cognizance as a head of lettuce.

Elena's eyes welled up. "Take care of her, Jaime. She's my sister."

I kissed her on the cheek, tasting her salty tears. "I will. I promise." I stroked her hair. "Now go."

After they left, I sat down on the bed. Elena had drawn the

blinds and the only light in the room were those seeping through the slats. It was eerily quiet. Hollow, like a cave. Just like the way I felt inside. Why is this happening to us? I wondered. Is it something I did? She did? Could this be my punishment for that incident with Pancho Sanchez?

I gazed down at Allison who in a fetal position looked completely vulnerable. Her hair had fallen on her face and I swept it aside. She reminded me of Marina...the night I rushed her to the hospital. As then, I felt thoroughly helpless.

I couldn't begin to imagine the suffering Allison was going through. At a tender age of twenty-two, she had lost two people she really cared about. First her father whose memory she still cherished. Now Francisco. I wondered if she would ever be the same.

◆◆◆

I stood on the hill and looked down at the dark figures milling on the grassy knoll. They were a subdued lot, all dressed in black, the women wearing veils that fell to their faces. I recognized some of them: Mildred holding the hand of her daughter Andrea, Ignacio who I was relieved to know hadn't been injured in the blast, and a few others who had sat with us during dinner. In front of the somber crowd lay three closed caskets gleaming in their blackness against the stark green of the lawn.

I bowed my head and murmured a little prayer. Don Pedro, Luis, and Andres. For one night, they came into our lives; painted our worlds. They would forever be burned in our memories. I stared blankly at my feet, holding back emotions that were threatening to spill out. Why did I feel so alone? In the kitchen that morning, I had asked Allison to come with me to the funeral but she made some vague excuse about not feeling well. Then without another word, she turned and walked back to her room. It had been typical of her attitude in the last few days.

A movement below brought me out of my reverie. Six men had now hunkered around the first casket and were lowering it into the pit. A rope had been wrapped around each end of the gleaming tube to stabilize its descent. I waited until all the caskets had been lowered then turned and made my way back to the train station.

◆◆◆

The police paid us a visit; two of them in civilian clothes. A greasy-faced man with a black mustache and a heavy browed detective with lots of hair on his face. They questioned everyone in the building: The Señora, Allison, Bjorn, Simone, myself, even Inaki and Jose Mari. No one was spared.

The greasy-faced detective interviewed me in the Senora's living room in front of two glasses of gaseosa and a pack of Habanos. He asked me all sorts of questions, like how well I knew Francisco, if I knew any of his friends or whether I knew of his activities in an organization called Lucha Por El Pais. He seemed particularly interested on our whereabouts on certain dates of the year. Why he keyed in on specific dates I could only speculate, but one of those dates happened to be the night a bomb blew a huge hole in the center of Algorda.

But in the end, they left us alone. That fact of the matter was, no one really knew much about Francisco's 'other' life.

On the morning after Don Pedro's funeral, I woke up at the usual time to have breakfast with Allison in the kitchen only to find she wasn't there. She had been asleep when I came home from the funeral the night before. Thinking her alarm clock might have acted up, I went over to wake her. "Allison?" I called, lightly rapping on the door.

Someone shuffled inside. The door swung open and Elena's sleepy eyes squinted at me through the opening.

"Oh hi Elena. Sorry to wake you." I peered over her shoulders. "Is Allison ready yet? It's getting kinda late."

Elena gave me a funny look. "I thought she was with you. She left an hour ago."

"Oh," I said. A rancid feeling rose up from the pit of my stomach. Oh God, don't do this to me.

In the days that followed, Allison avoided me like a nemesis. She went through lengths doing so. She took a different bus to work and changed her schedule to an earlier time so we wouldn't have to wait at the stop together. I tried to talk to her on several occasions, but I might as well have been talking to a tree. Her responses were as wooden as the desk in my room. "Yes," "No," "I have to go," were the extent of her responses to me. And when I pressed her for a reason why she was being so reticent, she had only shaken her head.

We still greeted each other in the hallway, but it was nothing more than a distant nod or a forced smile whereupon she would promptly slip into the bathroom or the bedroom or out the door for an easy escape. These carefully orchestrated acts were not lost to the other interns in the building.

"I'm sorry, Jaime," Elena would say after one of these episodes, after which she'd shake her head. She herself was at a loss for words.

Interestingly enough, Allison bounced back after only a few weeks. Chalk it up to the resiliency of youth. But her miraculous recovery did not in any way patch things between us. There was nothing to patch.

Eventually, she began to go out again; even dated men every now and then. Mostly friends she met at the university. I'd be lying if I said I wasn't hurt. Because I was, in a big way. But like her, I learned to deal with it.

I concentrated on work and became focused on my goals, a thing I had been neglecting lately due to my preoccupation with Allison. I learned the art of creative finance such as interest rate swaps and foreign exchange hedging. At last, I was getting into the meat of things. Mr. Joacquin showed me the intricacies of negotiation and took me along in his meetings with the bankers whose precious loans the company was becoming increasingly dependent on. I learned to execute money transfers and negotiate complicated letters of credit often in huge sums. To my amazement, I found that I had a natural skill for finance, so that during the latter part of my traineeship, I was left in charge of Mariposa's resources. Hundreds of millions of pesetas passed through my hands without my ever seeing a single peseta. I juggled money around like an elaborate ponzi scheme covering a wire transfer with other wire transfers so that by the end of the day I would come home frazzled and badly in need of a drink.

I worked hard during the day, and cliché as it might sound, played hard during the night, sometimes polishing off a bottle of Rioja wine to get over Allison who had drifted so far away from me we hardly even talked. Not lost to me was the fact that she might still be in love with me. It showed in the way she gazed at me from afar when she thought I wasn't looking and in the few times we bumped into each other in the hallway during which she would quickly look away almost in tears. We were estranged, yes. But lovingly estranged.

One night, I came home depressed. It was my birthday and no one knew about it. Wearily, I trudged up to my room and found a rectangular box sitting on my pillow. Gift-wrapped in shiny blue paper, it didn't have a card or anything that would suggest who had left it there. I lifted it curiously, turning it this way and that. Then carefully, I removed the wrapper. Inside was the shirt I had tried on at a shop at the Bertendon Gardens when Allison and I were coming back from lunch. I had wanted to buy it then, but thought better of it because of my finances.

I stared at it in disbelief. A bittersweet feeling pierced through my chest. She remembered, I thought, clutching the shirt to my chest. After all that had happened to us, she remembered.

On my way to the harbor that night, I thought of what the future held in store for me. I remembered what Allison said the day we had lunch at the Bertendon Gardens. "There is something out there, Jaime, waiting for us, ready to affect us in a big way. Just you and me. Maybe Elena too." I wondered if it would ever come true. And underneath all these musings came the question which had been festering in the back of my mind: *Why did Francisco have to die?*

☼ 15 Gemini

On the 20th day of July, five months to the day since setting foot in Bilbao, I stepped out of our apartment building and was confronted by an abandoned city. The buildings sat dark and the streets empty of people. I stood dumbfounded. Bilbao which not more than a week ago was a vibrant metropolis had become semi-moribund, its streets stripped of their usual color. Even the bars, the after-hour lifeline of our group, had shut their doors with signs posted on their windows that said, "Cerrado."

Dismayed by this turn of events, I ran up to complain to the Señora. She gave me a resigned shrug. "Ay chico," she said. "Eso es normal por aqui. Cada verano, todo del mundo se van para las vacaciones."

Apparently, towards the latter part of July and well into September, everyone in the city packs their bags and heads for the warmer climates of the Mediterranean. For the locals, this six week vacation binge might have been a gift from heaven, but for an extranjero like me who had come to expect my days filled with ardent interaction, this was a cause for gloom, for not only was there nothing to do in the godforsaken place but nothing to see. After all, a city without its people was nothing more than a collection of empty buildings.

But what depressed me even more than this feeling of abandonment was the looming threat that our traineeship was about to end, that we were living on borrowed time, and that soon, we would be heading our separate ways, leading separate lives, our friendships becoming nothing more than poignant memories soon to be forgotten. There was a finality about it that disheartened me, and when I looked upon it more closely, I realized that we really hadn't that much time left. Cliff's traineeship was concluding in a week, mine in two, the same with Miguel, Bjorn, Allison, and Simone. Elena, who like me had graduated from college, had planned on visiting relatives in Portugal before returning to Brazil. I was the only one whose future was unsettled, and every time the subject of leaving would come up, Allison would look at me in despair, and swiftly look away.

Those last two weeks were the gloomiest days in my life. Only a skeleton crew remained at Mariposa whose once tumultuous confines were now eerily mute. There wasn't enough work to go around. Everything had seemingly shut down. Even Mr. Joacquin who had volunteered to hold the fort for the benefit of the other *Jefes* was bored stiff. To pass the time, he would get up from his desk, visit the empty cubicles of his staff, fill out forms that didn't need filling, and sorrily return to his office only to stare at the polished surface of his desk.

One day, I asked him in not so many words how I had performed on the job.

"You've done great work here, Jaime," he responded. "I am very impressed with you. And considering we are only paying you sixteen thousand pesetas a month, I think we've got a good bargain."

I cleared my throat and crossed my fingers because I was about to ask him for a job.

"Mr. Joacquin, I know this may sound a little straightforward but I want to apply for a job here."

He stared at me pensively. "Why, you don't want to go back?"

"I am not going back, Mr. Joacquin. I had planned to stay, if not here then somewhere else."

He shook a Ducado from a pack and offered me one. We lit up. "I've already spoken to Saturnino about it," he said. "A month ago. I really want to keep you, Jaime. Unfortunately the company is not doing very well. Business is bad. España is in a mild recession. In fact, I will have to lay off some people." He shook his head. "If only this stupid recession would go away. I hate to lose such talent." He looked at me sympathetically. "I'm sorry Jaime."

My spirits sagged. The Mariposa job had been my only hope. Without it, I would have to tap into my savings, a measly five hundred dollars and the eighty thousand pesetas ($400) I had saved during the summer. After that what? Wander around Bilbao homeless and destitute?

My insecurities increased tenfold. I began to wonder if I would have the energy to overcome this setback given that I would be competing with displaced Spaniards who had every legitimate reason to work here. At that moment, it dawned on me that I was a man without a country; a man without a future. I was no better than the band of gypsies I met at the countryside.

I came home depressed.

"What's the matter, Jaime? You look so down," Elena said to me in the kitchen. She had just taken a shower and her dark hair was wet and slick.

"Mariposa won't extend my traineeship," I said.

She made a silent 'oh.' We had spoken about my situation before. She touched my arm. "You can come with me to Portugal. There'd be free rent there."

I forced a smile. "Thanks Elena. But I can't. I have to deal with this on my own."

"You'll keep it in mind though?"

"Yes. Of course." And because she was so sweet, I took her in my arms as one would a little sister unaware that Allison had been watching us. When we broke it off, it was too late. Allison was hastening back to the bedroom.

"Let me talk to her," Elena whispered.

Allison's actions didn't surprise me. Even though she had distanced herself from me, there was still a bond that existed between us, as if I still belonged to her, and she to me. I had long mused over this schizophrenic behavior on her part, about her wanting me and at the same time shunning me, and each time I did, I came away more confused. But it was this very trait drawing me to her, sweeping me off my feet. She was the most perfect imperfect woman I had ever met.

◆◆◆

That night, everyone gathered at the Cerveceria for a farewell dinner. Except for a smattering of people who had the hapless fate of remaining in Bilbao, we had the entire place to ourselves. We dragged several picnic tables together and under the shade of a huge oak tree feasted on eight rotisserie chickens, four pitchers of beer, and three bottles of wine. Miguel brought out his boombox and slid a flamenco tape in the slot.

With music humming in the background, we reminisced about old times and recaptured treasured memories, giggling at the vignettes we had all come to relish. But all it did was highlight the inevitable. We couldn't stop the clock.

Everyone became long-faced. Cliff, in a last ditch effort to lift our spirits said, "Hey, I know what. Why don't we all go on a trip to cap off the summer. Somewhere far."

"A trip? What a wonderful idea," Bjorn said. He glanced at Elena who nodded her head. "Where?" she asked.

"Castro Urdiales," Miguel said. "The Vagabonds are playing there in four days."

"The gypsy band from France? Hey, that's a great group." Elena.

All of a sudden, everyone was talking at the same time, putting in their two pesetas worth.

"And there will be a fiesta afterwards. We can all chip in for the food and drinks, and sleep on the beach at Laredo," Cliff said. He glanced at Miguel and said with meaning, "Under the stars." By then, their relationship had become an open window.

"Then we can go to Santander," Simone said, crossing her tan legs.

"Or down to Burgos to see the Gothic cathedral." Allison. Everyone had an idea of his own, so we tabled it for later discussion.

The next two days were spent preparing for the trip. Canned goods went into backpacks, sleeping bags were rolled into buns. Allison and Elena made the potato salad and bocadillos we would eat on the train.

On the day of the trip, we slung our backpacks on our shoulders and boarded a third-class train to Castro finding the cabins crowded with concert-goers. Cliff shared a seat with Miguel, Elena with Bjorn, Simone with a long-haired Swede she picked up at the train station, and inevitably, me with Allison. It was the first time since Francisco's death that we would be this close, and I was nervous. We sat in the back near the door to the connecting coach. I let her have the window seat.

We spent the first hour in awkward silence. Her proximity sent a warm glow along the sides of my arm.

I glanced at her obliquely and noted her classic features: her wealth of blond hair, her cherub face that I loved so much, the tanzanite eyes, her heart-shaped lips, and realized just how much I had missed her.

She closed her eyes, feigning sleep and I did the same for lack of a better thing to do. The train rumbled along pastures and rolling hills. We were halfway to Castro when Allison spoke. "I've lost too many friends, Jaime. People I loved." She said it so softly I thought I had imagined it. She opened her eyes and looked at me. "I'm a curse to men. They all die on me in the end." Her lips quivered. "God knows I never meant to hurt you. And when I see you so miserable because of me, I—I just want to die." She choked back the tears that were threatening to spill out. Her anguish tore at my heart, but I dared not say anything. She must let it out.

"I—I didn't tell you this, but I had a twin brother," she mumbled in between sobs.

Oh god, I thought.

She pushed her tears away. "His name was Andrew. We were very close. We could just about read each other's mind." She closed her eyes as if trying to call to mind some bitter-sweet memory. And for the first time in weeks, she smiled. "He even arranged some of my dates for me and they would always be perfect. As if I had chosen them myself.

"One night, we double dated and went to the senior prom. He didn't even want to go because he was preparing for an entrance exam to a private college. But I begged him to. We had never been to one before. It was wonderful. Our dates were perfect and we had so much fun."

She took a deep breath and a frown crossed her face. "But halfway through the party, this guy tried to force himself on me. He had a bad reputation in school, you know. Everyone was afraid of him because he was in a gang. He was suspended once for bringing a knife in class.

"Anyway, I said no to him, but I was very polite. I didn't want any trouble. I thought that if I was at least nice to him, he'd leave me alone." She bit her lower lip. "But it had exactly the opposite effect. He became obnoxious and continued ragging on me. Andrew stood up and told him to leave me alone. Mick stood there staring at us in front of everyone. I knew he wanted to attack Andrew, try to save face. But my brother was a big guy, you know, over six feet tall, and a tackle at the high school football team so he left."

Her lips trembled. "When the prom ended, I was nervous and kept looking around. The four of us were walking back to the car when they came out from behind a van. Mick and his friends. I was so scared. Not for me, but for Andrew. He was very stubborn. I tried to get him in the car but he stood his ground, ready to face them if he had to. I guess they didn't want to mess with him because Mick pulled out a gun and shot him in the face. Just like that. In cold blood." She shook her head. "If—if only I didn't ask him to the prom—maybe he'd still be alive." Her tears were now flowing, and it was then that I realized that no matter what I did to help her, no matter how hard I tried, nothing would ever make it right for her. The death of her father, then her twin brother, and now Francisco had probably so damaged her she would forever be vulnerable. She opened her eyes and looked at me. "So you see, Jaime, even though I longed to be with you, I—I can't let myself." She gazed out the window. "I don't want you to die on me. Just like my father did... and Andrew."

"Francisco too?"

"Francisco was a close friend, nothing else. I always wanted to tell you that. But yes, Francisco too."

This time, it was my turn to look away. I had felt the 'curse' too. Bad things seemed to happen when we're together. Maybe that was the reason why I ran away from her after Algorda. But even so, I was willing to take a chance.

"You are the most important thing in the world to me,

Allison," I said. "Nothing else matters. And if dying is a consequence of loving you, then I'd gladly risk it." It was a bold statement on my part, but I unequivocally believed it at the time. I took her hand. "Remember what you told me when we had lunch at Bertendon? That there's something out there waiting for us? Ready to affect us in a big way?"

She nodded.

"Don't you want to find out what it is?" I pressed her hand. "We can beat this Allison. You and me. We've already survived a lot of things." Her pupils broadened. I thought I might have gotten through to her. Even if only a little bit. And so as we sat there in silence with her leaning against me, I felt that we had somehow moved into the initial steps towards reconciliation. At least now we understood each other. And as if to reinforce this point, Allison put her head on my chest and encircled her arms around me. I had to be the happiest man alive at that moment, I felt such joy that I could have whooped up from my seat and pranced up and down the aisle in giddy exultation. Fragile as it might be, we had bridged the distance between us and forged a delicate compromise. I sighed contentedly, and stared out at the scenery. Orchards and poppy fields drifted by, then the first of Castro's white cottages.

The train let us off in an underground station at the center of town. Castro Urdiales, I discovered, was a small fishing village ninety kilometers west of Bilbao not unlike many small towns along the Basque coast. Quaint and picturesque, it was a settlement of whitewashed houses set against the backdrop of the Cantabrian mountains. Like Algorda, it was built on a jagged cliff, its structures sweeping down in precarious layers, but whereas Algorda was wealthier and newer in appearance,

Castro was more ancient, its buildings a flesh-tone pink from the mist and salt air drifting in from the sea. But it was this distinctly venerable appearance that gave it its charm.

We paused at a look out point with a sweeping view of Laredo, a collection of modern hotels and condominiums along an arcing band of sand and whistled at the sight. The water was a bright turquoise, so clear I could see the rocks at the bottom of it.

"It's beautiful," Allison exclaimed. She grabbed my arm. "Where are they going to hold the concert, do you know?"

"See that park over there?" Cliff said, biting into an apple he had snatched from Miguel's bag.

"That square thing outside of town with the trees around it?"

"Yes. I heard they're building the stage today. They should be finished with it in time for tomorrow's concert. There is supposed to be a laser show tonight."

"What are those boats doing there?" Simone pointed at a flotilla of barges floating far into the horizon. Allison, who had researched the attractions of the region before we left Bilbao said, "They're fishing boats. This used to be an old whaling port in the 14th century. The whales are gone but there's still a lot of squid and mackerel along the coast."

Later, after dumping our backpacks in a bar owned by Iñaki's cousin, Allison tugged on my arm. "I want to be alone. Take a walk with me?"

She wanted to see the Iglesia de San Martin at the adjacent town, a Gothic cathedral built by the Christians, renovated by the Moors, and later reconstructed by the Christian Moors after having been severely damaged in battle. Up until that time, I didn't know there was such a thing as a Christian Moor, it sounded oxymoron. And yet, the story had it that the Moriscos as the Spanish Moors were known, after centuries of imposing their will on Spain, eventually succumbed to the Christian faith and built themselves a church.

It was a long way to the cathedral, a hike which took us through the old whaling stations along the harbor complete with its salt-eroded barges and giant hooks, past the whimsical gardens of Parque de Santilles with its copper statue of a Spanish horseman, across the arching bridge of Rio Basauri, into a tree-lined cobblestone path leading to the basilica. The cathedral, lavender in color, was both Gothic and Moorish at the same time, as if its builders had been confused as to what exactly they had in mind when they built it. Facing the road were Gothic steeples of the most intricate kind I had ever seen, each one sculpted into flamboyant cone-like shapes, and arranged according to graduating height with the tallest steeple in the center. This was connected to the body of the main church, a barn-like structure of faded sandstone so devoid of style it almost looked ugly next to its princely counterpart, and from here, one could traverse into the walled-in garden of the rectory lush with low growing trees and shrubbery at the end of which was a Moorish bell tower, again made of sandstone, soaring up ten stories capped by a rounded turret.

"Francisco said if you climbed up to that tower, you can see all of Santander."

"How would he know that?"

"He's from this province."

The only way up was through a spiral staircase barely wide

enough to accommodate one person, and we had to duck at every landing where the ceiling stooped low, making the upward trek disastrous on the back. It was three hundred steps of uneven slabs which were not only slippery but also steep so that by the time we reached the top, we were gasping for breath.

As promised, the tower offered a sweeping view of the Cantabria, and from our vantage point, we could see along this great Basque coastline sandy beaches stretching out for miles towards Santander, past the Santilla del Mar, and the little coastal towns of Costa Verde. Allison at once hugged me. I could never describe just how good that hug felt, for I needed her so badly more than life itself. It was better than sex, food, and drugs put together. "Oh God, it has been so long," she whispered fervently. "I love you so much, Jaime. So much." We stayed that way for a few minutes. While we had never formally acknowledged a commitment to each other, we made a conscious effort not to hold back, and to let things simply happen. I for one wanted a more definite relationship, but I sensed in Allison a hesitation to do so, so I let it go. After all, what difference did it make? At least we were together.

She shivered in my arms. "What is it?" I asked.

"I'm afraid."

I fell silent.

"What will become of us, Jaime?"

"I—I don't know." And because we both felt lost, we held onto each other like little kids in the dark.

"I want to visit Francisco's aunt. She lives around here," Allison said.

"What for?"

"I have to find out what happened to him, Jaime, or I'll never put his death to rest." She sighed. "If I only knew he was in trouble, I might have been able to help him."

I took her hand, tugged at it gently. "You couldn't have done anything, Allison. His problem went much deeper than that." I debated whether to tell her about seeing Francisco at the Algorda plaza. It had been eating at me since the night of the explosion. "Remember when we were at the plaza with Mildred and Don Pedro?"

"Yes..." Her face took on a fearful cast. My resolve wavered. "We were sitting with Mildred..."

She paled.

"I saw him walk by with two men, Allison. He was carrying a bag..."

"Jaime, how could you insinuate that..."

"I'm not insinuating anything. I'm just telling you what I saw."

A look of guilt crossed her face and for a moment, I thought she was going to break down in tears. "I—I thought I saw him too," she said deflatedly.

"You what?"

She nodded. "I didn't want to spoil our evening so I didn't call him. But maybe if I did..."

"Allison, stop. It's not your fault. Nor mine. We saw him, we suspected him, but that doesn't mean he did it." I was beginning to understand her reticent behavior. She had borne the guilt all this time.

"That's why I want to see his aunt. To put this thing to bed. She raised him, you know."

While I wasn't anxious about meeting Francisco's aunt and

rehashing all those painful events, I would do it ten times over if it would free Allison of her guilt. "Where does she live?"

"In the hills above Santander. At a small village called Ibanez."

☼ 16 Curse of the Gypsy Moth

Ibanez was a fifty-minute bus ride from Castro. After queuing the group of our special trip to see Francisco's aunt, we boarded a red bus that would take us over the mountains to Santander. For the first time since we met, we were truly alone. No apartment to go back to, no pressing commitments to keep.

It was a strange feeling traveling together on a bus in a country neither one of us knew much about. We found comfort in each other's company. Allison grabbed my hand.

"Are you feeling what I'm feeling?" she asked.

I looked at her and nodded. I wondered if this was how it felt like to be married. Two people as one. It was an idea not hard for me to imagine.

The bus took us through the ragged mountainside, weaving through magnificent canopies of fir and cypresses, and at times, when the road was free of the obstructing overhang, we would see the blue waters of the coast sparkling in the sunlight.

The bus dropped us off in the center of a resort town much more modern than any I had ever seen. The buildings were new and uniform in height, by my estimation no more than five or six stories, set against a wide strip of beach which at this time of the day teemed with people. While I found the town delightfully clean and a welcome respite from the filth of Bilbao, there was an antiseptic quality about it that didn't appeal to me; everything seemed to have been planned too fastidiously for my taste. The absence of alluring old architecture made it doubly so.

Seeing my reaction, Allison said, "There was a big fire here several years ago. The entire city burned down. They had to rebuild it from ground up."

We didn't know what type of reception we would get from Francisco's aunt, we were both strangers to her. In all likelihood, she would welcome us with open arms since we were coming as friends of her dead nephew, but one could never tell.

It was with this feeling of unease that we climbed the flight of stairs that would take us to the top of the hill upon which the sleepy town of Ibanez lay. The uphill path wormed us through terraced orchards and gardens and neat little lookout points awash with roses and hydrangea blossoms. It was a grueling climb and we had to make numerous stops along the way to catch our breath.

In one of the stops, we came upon a small vendor stand under the shade of a walnut tree behind which sat an unusual looking man with blond hair so fair it looked almost white. His eyes were pink, and his skin, nearly translucent. He was short, no more than four foot three, and it was only when he came up close that we realized he was an albino. A pushy albino. He had a lot to sell, from cartons of Ducados and assorted bottled drinks to exotic cheeses and dried meats. He had knickknacks of every sort, bushels of them: nuts, bolts, dental picks, screw drivers, magnifying glass—you name it.

His stand was made of wood, no more than ten feet by ten feet, topped by an aluminum roof whose eves were adorned with a thin growth of spotted ivy. I noticed a small cot sticking out from behind a Turkish curtain at the rear section of the stand, leading me to believe that he might be living there.

"Ah, extranjeros. Come, come. I have a lot of things for you to see," he said in a whiny voice.

"We really just want some gaseosa," I said, pointing at the bottle of mineral water on the counter.

"But you must see what I have, señor. I have a lot of things, especially for your beautiful señorita." He grabbed Allison's hand and led her inside, pulling out a wooden valise from under the cot. Setting it on the table, he opened the lid and revealed a glittering assortment of jewelry.

Among his collection included a pair of turquoise earrings set in filigree silver, copper coin necklaces of every size and length, a silver nose ring he claimed to have purchased from a descendant of Cachondo, and all sorts of handcrafted bangles and beads. From a pouch, he pulled out a black leather bracelet with six Moorish beads and held it up under the sunlight. "This was from my beautiful cousin Nimfa," he said. He gave an exaggerated sigh as he admired its beauty, and whenever the sun's rays touched upon the beads, they would sparkle like specks of gold.

"Hey, what's in those beads," I asked, squinting at them.

"Cordoban gold. They are embedded in the beads to create the design. Nimfa made it herself."

"They're beautiful," Allison said.

"The design is Indic and means lost love."

"Lost love," Allison repeated. "But who is Nimfa?"

The albino motioned to a bench and handed us two tumblers. He fished out a large bottle of gaseosa from a cooler, popped off its cap, and poured each of us a drink. The liquid bubbled over.

"I'm a gypsy, do you know that?" the albino said.

I looked at him doubtfully and shook my head.

"Well I am. I happen to be an albino so I don't look like one."

"But what are you doing here? Aren't you supposed to be with your caravan?"

He rolled his eyes. "Because I am an albino, that's why. I was shunned by my tribe so I left it. There were those who said that I should have stayed. That I shouldn't have paid attention to all the badgering. My cousin Nimfa would have agreed with them. God, she was so beautiful."

"Where is she now?"

"She is dead. Her brother Alejandro killed her."

Allison gulped. "Her brother?"

The albino stared at her, then at me. "I tell you this because you may be faced with a similar situation later."

Perplexed, Allison and I looked at each other.

"Nimfa," the albino began, "was the princess of the tribe. She was so beautiful all the gypsy men were after her from the time she turned twelve. She developed early, you see, and blossomed into a desirable young woman."

He took a stick of Habanos and lit up. Smoke curled out of his nose and danced along the eaves. "But in all those years, she managed to ward them off. She didn't think it was time to fall in love, you see. She liked boys, but only as friends.

"Well, one of the men in love with her was Orgullo, the best friend of Alejandro, Nimfa's brother. Orgullo's family was rich and the leader of a related tribe. They owned Arabian stallions and had lots of gold and jewelry.

"Because of this, Alejandro wanted to be part of Orgullo's family. So he devised a plan: He'd marry Orgullo's sister. He thought that by doing so, he would be able to unite the families and get his hands closer to the gold." A blue jay landed on the orange tree in front of us and started squawking. Annoyed, the albino threw a rock at it. He muttered a curse under his breath before turning back to us.

"The only problem was, Orgullo wouldn't let him unless Alejandro convinced Nimfa to marry Orgullo as well. Alejandro didn't like it at first because it would complicate his plans. But then he thought that it would make the bond stronger. Then everybody would be happy."

"You mean he's going to force Nimfa into an arranged marriage?" Allison scoffed.

"We are Gypsies, señorita. It is perfectly normal for marriages to be done in such a fashion. Anyway, the two men made a pact. Orgullo would convince his father that Alejandro was the right man for his sister, while Alejandro did the same."

Allison muttered something under her breath. I smiled.

The albino continued, "Everything was going as planned.

They had convinced both patriarchs that it was the right thing to do. They even set a date for the double wedding, which was to be on Nimfa's fifteenth birthday.

"Except something happened. During their pilgrimage south that year, Nimfa met a man at the carnival in Santander and fell in love. He wasn't Gypsy. In fact, he wasn't even Spanish. He was an American who worked at a food company in town. They met at the fortune telling booth when he was having his fortune told by Nimfa's aunt.

"Love must have struck them hard because in the following days, they sneaked out into the plains to be alone." The albino took another puff of his cigarette. "On the third night they were to meet, Alejandro saw Nimfa slipping out of camp with the American.

"He followed them. In his fist was a hunting knife with which to kill them if Nimfa's honor was compromised."

"Isn't that a little bit extreme?" I said skeptically.

"No señor. Because according to Gitano tradition, a woman must be a virgin on the eve of her nuptial or she would be forsaken by her husband to be. That would have ruined Alejandro's plan. Fortunately, they spent most of the time talking and holding hands. They didn't even go beyond kissing.

"At any rate, that night, Alejandro confronted Nimfa in front of the entire family and told her in no uncertain terms that she had disgraced the family's honor by consorting with an extranjero. I was there. I saw it and it was terrible. *How could you bring shame to this family*, Alejandro castigated. *He is not even a Gypsy.*

"And so to preserve the family's honor, the chieftain forbade Nimfa to see the American anymore. But the chieftain refused to cut short their stay in Santander. He reasoned that the carnival was about to end anyway and they would soon be on their way, avoiding further complications to the marriage plans.

"During their remaining days in town, they assigned an aunt to guard Nimfa. Just to keep the American away. It was pure hell for the poor niña. Can you imagine? There she was, seeing her lover and not being able to be with him."

Something made me turn to Allison who blushed and pressed my hand.

"Anyway, Nimfa wanted to give the American something to remember her by, so she made him this bracelet. On our last night in Santander, she asked me to give it to him along with a note. She was my favorite cousin so I agreed. After all, what harm could it do?

"That night, I handed the note to the American and realized I had left the bracelet in the tent. I told him to wait and went back to get it. By the time I came back, the American was gone. Nimfa found a way to slip out of the tent, you see. Apparently, the note had asked the American to meet her in this very spot we are now sitting. She figured no one would follow them up here and they could both hide in the hills until the caravan left." He poured himself some gaseosa.

"So what happened to them?" Allison prompted.

"Orgullo saw her slip away in the direction of the hills and immediately told Alejandro. As you can imagine, Alejandro got very angry. He marched to his tent and came back with the dagger."

"Oh no," Allison said.

"Unfortunately yes, señorita. And this time, he was going to put a stop to this nonsense. He took off after them in the hills and found them making love in that spot right there." The albino pointed to a patch of grass under a grove of orange trees. "Alejandro was so mad that he dragged the American away from Nimfa and beat him up with the help of Orgullo. But they didn't kill him. They were smart enough not to do that because they knew he would be missed. Instead, they ordered him down the stairway to Santander and threatened to kill him if he ever came back."

"What happened to Nimfa?" I asked.

"They raped her. First Alejandro, and then Orgullo, then Alejandro again."

"But she was his sister," Allison protested.

"Yes, señorita, but she had soiled herself in his eyes and deserved what she got."

"Did she report them to the police?"

"A Gypsy reporting another Gypsy to the police? You must be kidding, señorita. There is no such thing in a Gypsy custom."

"So what happened to her?"

"She grabbed Alejandro's knife and killed herself. At least that was what Alejandro said. But I had long suspected that it was the other way around. That he killed her so the father wouldn't find out about the rape. The only reason I know is that Orgullo bragged about it one time to his cousin who is also my cousin."

"But wouldn't the police go looking for her after the American reported it?" I said.

"Yes, and they did. But Alejandro had gotten rid of the

body. I heard they cut her up in little pieces and served her at the carnival."

I grimaced. Allison looked like she was about to be sick.

The albino shook his head "Alejandro is like a *moth*, you see. He destroys everything he touches." He stared at us. "But that's not the point of the story. The reason I am telling you this is that the two of you are in a similar situation. You're different from each other, yes? There are times when you will be tested, just like Nimfa and the American. But love is always stronger, no matter the consequences. Nimfa knew the dangers, yet she did what she had to do. That is life."

I wondered how many times he had told the story for the purpose of selling 'Nimfa's' bracelet. For all I knew, he could have hundreds of them under his cot. But true or not, his 'sales talk' worked. I gave him five hundred pesetas for the bracelet and hooked it around Allison's wrist. A ray of sunlight shone on the 'gold' filling. "With this bracelet, I thee wed," I said jokingly. Allison blushed. She thanked me with a kiss. "I'll always treasure this, Jaime. No matter what happens." I nodded to her. I felt sad. Our time together was steadily dwindling away. September was just around the corner.

The albino cleared his throat, muttering something about nature's call. He turned and marched in the direction of the woods, leaving us alone on the bench. We took advantage of the time to kiss and hold hands and as we were doing so, I couldn't help but feel that we were living in some sort of a romantic tragedy where everything was poignant and bittersweet with fate waiting in the wings to tear us apart. No, I thought. I won't let it happen. Like the Gypsy said, love is always stronger.

When the albino came back ten minutes later, we had finished the gaseosa.

"Ready?" I asked Allison.

She nodded. I turned to the albino. "Thanks for the bracelet. We never knew your name."

"El Rubio," he said. The blond man. "Vaya con Dios."

☼17 The Waxing Moon

Hand in hand, we puffed the rest of the way up, trying to get our bearings in the maze of pathways that split off into several directions, and each time we encountered one of these forks, we would always take the high road. The vegetation grew thick, blanketing the walkway with overhang so dense it gave us the illusion of being in a forest. There was a winter-green smell in the air tinged with the odor of moss and compost.

The trail dropped us off in front of a wrought iron arch welded with the word *Ibanez* in black Gothic lettering, and from this arch, we could see the sleepy town in one sweeping glance: eight or ten false-fronted structures on four short streets surrounded by a scattering of cottages along the cliffs. The sky had darkened into a rich ultramarine. The sun, now an orange sliver, peeked over the rooftops.

I noticed that the town had no paved roads, only uneven

paths too narrow for cars to pass through, but wide enough for horses to trot on. In the center of town was a plaza, and this too was landscaped in dirt, but made picturesque by a generous growth of shade trees and a man-made lake upon which floated a flock of long-necked swans.

A game of bocci was in progress in the plaza, the competitors, bent old men in black berets seemingly too old even for this sedentary activity. Each one of them could hardly bend down, let alone roll the ball. I felt we had inadvertently stepped into a time warp and landed in another decade earlier in the century.

Allison shivered. I pressed her hand reassuringly. "Let's go to a bar and ask the bartender for directions."

There was only one bar in town, a one-story building with a green facade on which was a wooden sign declaring *Octavio's Bar* in peeling letters and it was here that we encountered a bartender so old his face looked like parchment paper blemished with wide blotches of age spots, and each time he wiped the counter with a wet rag, his hands shook so badly I was tempted to take the rag from him and do the job myself. But he was lucid, and had a surprisingly clear voice.

"Ah si, Señora Giron. She lives in the pink house at Camino Oso on the other side of the plaza."

"What number?" I asked hopefully.

He wagged a veined finger at me. "We don't have street numbers in Ibanez, chaval. Just look for the pink house." I glanced at Allison who gave me the *it's getting stranger by the minute* look. And so here we were in this spooky little town, all weirded out but trying to maintain a brave face, searching for a house without a number to visit a woman we had never met.

We walked across the plaza and gave a half-hearted wave to the old men with the bocci balls who at that moment, had decided to take a break from this seemingly strenuous game to watch us walk by. From the intensity of their stares, they obviously found us more entertaining than the bocci, and I could just imagine them asking each other what had prompted a beautiful *rubia* and an exotic-looking *morenito* to grace their humble little town.

We were soon lost underneath the trees, following a trail called Camino Oso, and it was only when we reached the end of the cul-de-sac did we come across the pink house. It was not as small as I had imagined for a town of Ibanez's size. In fact, it was rather large, boasting two majestic stories of light pink stucco, a red tile roof, and black-grilled balconies at each window.

The entire lot, green and pastoral, was bordered by a ten-foot hedge whose top had been sheared into imaginative ornamental shapes, and all we could see from the street were the arcaded terraces and part of the patio visible through the gate.

There seemed to be an abundance of birds in Ibanez; we could hear their persistent chirping everywhere. The gate was open so we invited ourselves in, rather uneasily, and found ourselves in the middle of a brick patio shadowed by the overarching branches of flowering crepe myrtles.

The cry of the violin floated softly from inside the house, accenting its already rustic setting, and as we drew nearer the front door, we caught a whiff of cooking meat so appetizing I found myself salivating. If my nose hadn't failed me, I thought I detected garlic and basil, and maybe a dash of rosemary.

Allison rang the doorbell, and reached her hand out to me for comfort. It took a few seconds before a middle-aged woman answered the door. "Si?" the woman asked.

"Señora, my name is Allison Flynn. I'm a friend of Francisco."

The woman's eyes widened as if she remembered the name. "Ah si, si, Allison. Francisco had spoken of you."

"And this is my friend Jaime," Allison continued.

A smile creased the woman's face.

"Who is it Tia?" A girl came to the door. She couldn't have been more than ten or eleven, but she was very pretty. I, at once, saw her resemblance to Francisco.

"This is Francisco's sister, Maria," the woman said. "And I am Señora Giron."

We smiled at the girl who blushed and hugged her aunt's arm.

"Oh, how rude of me," Señora Giron said. "Won't you come in?"

She walked us into a room furnished with heirloom furniture so old it could have come straight from a palace in medieval Spain, and when she motioned for us to sit, I hesitated ever so slightly, fearing of inflicting damage to the delicate chairs.

She sat down in front of us with her hands primly on her lap. Maria sat beside her. I imagined there was another person in the house, for I could hear a clatter in the kitchen: the stirring of pots, the clanging of pans. As if reading my thoughts, Señora Giron turned to Maria. "Ayuda la Señora Valencia, chiquita," after which, the little girl stood up and walked obediently into the kitchen.

Señora Giron turned to us. "You want to know about Francisco," she said, getting to the heart of the matter.

"Yes Señora," Allison said.

"Did the policia tell you why he was killed?"

"No Señora."

"They didn't come to see you?"

"They did, Señora. But they only asked questions," Allison said.

Señora Giron nodded. "I thought so. Bueno, I'll tell you. But it is a long story. Are you staying in Santander?"

We looked at each other. "No Señora," Allison said. "We didn't plan on coming here until a couple of hours ago."

"Then you must stay for the night."

We were about to politely decline when she said, "I insist. It is what Francisco would have wanted. But first, we must eat, yes?" Without waiting for an answer, she called out to the kitchen. "Nos vamos a cenar, Valencia."

When we came out, dinner was waiting for us at the patio. The table was set for four. A pair of candelabras gave a wavering light on the table, punctuating a lacey tablecloth of fine silk.

The meal began with a prayer and I found myself holding hands with Maria and Allison, reciting Spanish incantations I had long ago learned as a child. Señora Valencia served the food in dainty ceramic plates, the fare comprising of a steaming bowl of pinto bean soup, rice pilaf, filete de corderito or lambchops, green verduras, and caramelized flan. Not having eaten a home-cooked meal for some time, Allison and I gorged on the food, to the detriment of our good manners. Señora Giron watched us with amusement.

"You are exchange students, no?"

We both nodded with our mouths full.

She sighed. "So innocent. So unaware of the political situation in the Vascongadas." She was saying it almost to herself. "I am only glad the police left you alone. You two came all the way from Bilbao?"

"No Señora. Our friends are waiting for us in Laredo for a concert," Allison said.

"And yet you took the time for a special trip to find out about Francisco," the Señora said. We both nodded, and continued eating. She seemed pleased with that.

The dinner took an hour after which, the Señora led us with our anisettes to the living room. She started off by saying, "I'm the sister of Francisco's mother. I raised Francisco and his brother Juan, and of course, la chiquitina," referring to Maria, the little one.

"The family used to be a normal one. My sister was happily married, she had a handsome husband who treated her well, and they were quite well off. And, of course, they had the children. Three beautiful ones." She took a framed photograph from the table and handed it to Allison. "Francisco was the eldest and the favorite of his mother. Juan, the one holding the soccer ball in that picture, was two years younger. And of course you have Maria who was but a child then. You might wonder why I am raising the children."

She looked at us for confirmation, but didn't wait for an answer. "You see, the children lost their parents early on. Francisco's father was a rich business man. He had a company in Bilbao that manufactured tractor tires and spare parts. He is also well connected to the Madrid government. He was always in the news, rubbing elbows with the King's family." She waved a vague hand at the room. "This house, it was only their vacation home. They had others in Santander and Bilbao."

Allison nodded. "I have been to the one in Bilbao. It was very big although Francisco liked the dormitories better. I've asked him about his parents, but he wouldn't tell me."

Señora forced a smile. "Francisco is very secretive about his parents. And we seldom go to that house except during the school year to visit him. We like it better here in Ibanez where it is sheltered from all the politics of Spain." There was a bitterness in her voice. "You see, nine years ago, my sister and her husband went on a vacation to Biarritz. It was to be their second honeymoon. They called me at my cottage at Castro Urdiales and asked me to babysit the children for a couple of weeks. Francisco was only twelve then, and Juan ten.

"On the way to Biarritz, Francisco's father decided to stop in Bilbao to take care of business at the factory and to let his foreman know that they were leaving for France. He made a few phone calls, paid a few bills, spoke to his lawyer, and gave the foreman last minute instructions about work."

She paused pensively, as if deciding how to proceed. "Bear in mind, niños, that those were tumultuous times in the Vacongadas, more so than now. ETA was killing government officials on whim, and those they suspected as 'collaborators' to Madrid's cause.

"Because of this, I had asked my brother-in-law to hire a bodyguard on a number of occasions, but he was very much against the idea. He didn't consider himself different from the

Basques. In fact, he sympathized with them and made it a point to give them work in his factory. You see, even though he associated with royalty, he was naive when it came to politics. He always believed that if you treated people well, there would be a way to reconcile the differences. That day, as they were driving out of the factory's gate, a car exploded in the street. The explosion consumed all the vehicles along the block including theirs."

"Oh my Lord," Allison said.

"What happened to the children?" I asked.

"Francisco was beside himself. He threw things on the wall and crushed a statue of Jesus Christ with a hammer." At this, she made a sign of the cross. "He wept that entire week, unwilling to accept his parents' death. But he knew he had to be strong for Juan and Maria, so he straightened out. I tried to raise the children as my own and I think I succeeded to a certain extent. I gave them love, and a good home. It was difficult, not having a husband to help raise them, but it was worth all the love."

I took a sip of anisette. "Francisco must have crossed the line somewhere."

"Yes, he did. For years, he hid his anger from me. I only found out about it because of his reaction to the news whenever another innocent victim was claimed by ETA. I remember him storming out of the den the day the mayor of Madrid was assassinated. It was as if the boy was consumed by rage. That's why I became concerned when he enrolled at Universidad de Deusto. It would put him too close to the people he hated. Do you understand?"

"Yes Señora."

"I tried to convince him to attend Salamanca. It is a good university, but he wanted to learn business, and Deusto is one of the best business schools in the country. Remember, the factory is still his and he wanted to run it. He had a good sense for it too." She smiled fondly at the memory.

"And you know what? For years he was able to live with his enemies. It is true that he formed a pro-Madrid organization at school, but it was a non-violent organization. Only meant to educate the Bilbainos that Madrid wasn't an enemy. At the time, I thought that he had overcome his demons. That is, until a year ago." She turned to Allison. "Did he tell you about Juan?"

"No, Señora. He spoke of you and Maria, but never of Juan."

Señora Giron nodded. "He wanted to forget."

"Forget what, Señora?" Allison asked.

"You see, Juan was in the military. All Spanish men are required by law to attend military training. Juan was a good typist so he was assigned a desk job at the Ayuntamiento in Bilbao. At the time, we thought how lucky he was for having escaped the grueling exercises of the actual field training. But one day, General Vargas, the commander of the Guardia Civil, visited the Governor at the Ayuntamiento. It was a well-publicized meeting because it involved a debate on whether to grant Vizcaya limited autonomy. The General was very much against it.

"ETA set a trap for him. They waited outside city hall and opened-fire from three sides as he got into his car. It was lunch time. Juan was about to meet Francisco at the university. He was hit in the crossfire."

Jesus, I thought. Allison wrung her fingers.

"Francisco got very secretive after that," the Señora said. "He would bring friends home but they were not the type of people he should be associating with. I warned him about them many times but he wouldn't listen." Señora Giron sighed. "I guess you know that he was suspected of bombing Algorda."

Allison bowed her head.

"We were both there, Señora," I said. "We saw the whole thing. Some of the people with us were killed."

"Jesu Cristo. I'm so sorry."

"But...do you believe them, Señora? You think he did it?"

She stared at me. "My heart wanted to say no. But there was so much hatred in him. And you saw him, didn't you?"

I sighed my acknowledgement. "I thought I did but I wasn't sure. I could have been mistaken. It was dark, and very crowded, but he was with this guy with long hair."

"Yes, that's Roberto. He was expelled from the army for stealing guns. He was killed too." The Señora turned to Allison. "Now, does this convince you that you couldn't have done anything to save him? Francisco's fate had been set for him long before you two knew each other." How she read Allison's mind, I had no way of knowing, but I had a feeling she had us pegged from the moment we introduced ourselves.

Allison sat with her head bowed.

"Pobrecita. How you must have suffered," the Señora said, taking Allison in her arms. "I would be happier if you freed yourself of this guilt, Allison. It is not your fault."

We finished our anisettes then the Señora stood up. "Now you must rest. You were probably traveling all day."

She ushered us up a bannistered stairway to the guest bedrooms at the rear of the house where we wouldn't be disturbed by the kitchen noise. She stepped into a half-lit room. "This will be yours, Allison. There are extra blankets in the closet if you get cold." She turned on the lamp; absently looked around. "This used to be Maria's room," she said.

"Thank you, Señora," Allison said. "You are so kind."

"It is the least I can do. You took this special trip because he was your friend." She gave Allison a hug. Turning to me, she said, "Let me show you to your room, Jaime."

◆◆◆

I opened the sliding glass door; relished the cool breeze. Santander glimmered in the distance, its broad strip of beach blazing under the spotlights. Farther on, out in the prussian blue darkness flickered the lights of the merchant ships.

I took a deep breath, pondering on the day's events: the train ride from Bilbao, getting back with Allison, the trip to Ibanez; Señora Giron...her stories about the family. Francisco. Now that I heard his story, I sympathized with the man. He would have turned out a different person had those things not happened to his family. In a sense, he and Allison were so much alike. Maybe that was what drew them together. Both had lost people they loved, both had suffered because of it, both had let the tragedies rule their lives. And as I was contemplating over this, I realized how much I wanted to cherish Allison, shelter her from further misery. She was so vulnerable. The impression I had of her when I first arrived in Bilbao had been entirely off-kilter. I had thought then that she was a haughty young woman who used men and spat them out. She turned out to be exactly the opposite.

Instinctively, I glanced at the partition wall and felt a stir of excitement. She's in there, I thought. Waiting. An agonizing heat scorched through my loins. My heart began to pound.

Weak-kneed, I padded to the door, placed my head against it. Nothing. Only silence. I opened the door a crack. Dark. A rushing river rumbled in my ears. Quietly, I stepped into the hallway. Allison was waiting for me at the door, still completely dressed. Without a word, she came into my arms. Her kiss was wet, urgent. I felt her tugging on my neck, my hair. When we broke it off, she was panting heavily.

I slipped out of my jacket, threw it on a chair. My hands trembled as I led her to bed. It was the first night we would be alone together, in the same room, on the same bed. We had kissed, we had held hands, we had embraced with great emotion, but we had never made love.

For a fleeting moment, we sat on the mattress, neither talking, neither touching. Then shyly, we slipped out of our clothes and slid under the covers.

Her body was soft as she snuggled into my arms seeking warmth. She kissed my neck. "Thank you for taking me here, Jaime. I'm glad we came."

I nodded. I could feel her ample breast pressing against my ribs.

"Do you love me?" she asked softly. She had never asked that before.

"Yes. Very much"

She stroked my chest. "It's strange. The way we met. The things that happened to us." Her finger caressed my nipple.

I tried to hold down my excitement that was now pushing against her belly but it seemed to grow even harder. She brought her hands down and stroked it. "You're excited," she whispered. I leaned over, kissed her. Her tongue swept across mine. When she broke away, she said, "I want you to know I never slept with him."

I nodded. It wasn't important. What she did before 'us' was irrelevant.

We caressed each other for a few moments before she spoke again. "I'm a virgin, Jaime," she said, somewhat embarrassed. "I mean—don't get me wrong—I'm not a prude or anything—it's just that I haven't found the right man."

"Shhh Allison, you don't have to explain. It's nothing to be ashamed of." I got up on my elbows. "Am I the right man?"

She stared at me for a long time as though trying to frame an answer to a difficult question, and it was only after she had thoroughly thought about it that she nodded.

"You hesitated."

"It's just that we only have three weeks left. I don't know if we're doing the right thing."

"We don't have to do it Allison," I said gently.

"But I want to," she whispered.

I treated her tenderly. Like a delicate flower. Her body was soft, open to the touch, and as I brought my lips to her breasts giving her nipples a gentle bite, I felt a roaring in my ears. She was moaning now, twisting and squirming under me. I traced my lips down to her navel, licking around the soft depression, then followed the gentle cleft along her belly to the patch of blond hair below. She was a bountiful fountain, wet and musky, inciting an animal lust in me that was both free and suffocating.

"Now Jaime," she whispered.

I pulled myself up. Our movements were slow, deliberate, generating utmost bliss. I traced my hands along her curves, kneaded the softness of her skin, so smooth, like the mellow hills of the earth. They meandered endlessly, swelled sensuously, I found myself smothering in their richness. Then it happened. The jolt, the excruciating pain deep in my loins, the frenetic squirming. She pulled at my hair, sank her teeth lightly into my shoulders. We were gone.

Later, as we lay in each other's arms completely satiated, she whispered, "You're the sweetest man I had ever met, Jaime. I never thought it could be so wonderful." She kissed my neck and snuggled closer. We stayed in each other's arms, half dozing, half dreaming. I was falling into a slumber when I heard a cry of alarm.

"Wh—what's the matter?" I asked sleepily.

She was sitting up in bed, staring at the spots of blood on the sheets. "Señora Giron will see the stain," she said, distraught. Darting into the bathroom, she came out with a wet towel and vigorously scrubbed the blood off the fabric. She didn't stop until she had rubbed out all traces of it.

I felt bad. I had taken something away from her that she obviously valued.

◆◆◆

I woke up the next morning with the sun shining through the French doors. It bathed me with its gentle rays. I got up on my elbows and gazed down at Allison, fast asleep like a fair princess. God, I love her so. I felt a glow in my chest and was overcome by a giddy sensation. Everything was so dreamy, unreal. Once again, I thought about fate. What was it that brought me here; to this country, to this house on a hill, to this very room with the sun shining through the window, to this woman who now slept beside me. There must have been a reason. Gently, I stroked her hair, kissed her warm cheeks, then got up from the bed to gaze at the coastline. I felt exhausted, but wonderfully exhausted.

"Beautiful morning," a voice said behind me.

I turned, smiled. "Yes, it is."

She had sat up in bed with sheets wrapped around her. Her legs dangled over the side of the bed. She ran a hand through her hair, wriggled her toes, and I thought, deja vu.

"Just like our first morning, huh?" she said with a smile.

"Yes." I lifted her from the bed. "Except I couldn't touch you then."

"Oh, by the way, I got this for you." She reached for her purse and handed me a business card.

"What is it?"

"My boss's phone number. He's the controller at the bank. I mentioned you to him. That thing about the Lubricus. How you saved Mariposa tons of money. He's really interested."

My eyes widened.

"He wants you to call him in a month. He's forming an import-export financial subsidiary."

"Allison..." I began, and got all choked up. It was the most wonderful thing anyone had ever done for me. I looked at the card, thought about the timing of it, and it quickly occurred to me that even as we were having all those problems, she had kept my best interest at heart.

We made love one more time, showered together, then came down with our hair still wet. Señora Giron was waiting for us in the living room.

She smiled. "Buenos dias. Did you sleep well?"

"Si, Señora," Allison said. A blush had crept up on her face. "Gracias."

"Well, breakfast is ready." She ushered us to the patio where the maid Valencia was setting down a basket of steaming pastries. As we drank our coffee in large rounded mugs with sunlight seeping through the trees, the Senora said, "So, what will you be doing now?"

We shrugged. We didn't know.

She studied us for a moment and shook her head. "Ay niños, you're so innocent. You pretend there is nothing you can do about your love. But there are actually many many things. All you have to do is want it." Allison smiled at me.

"But also remember that España is an enchanted land. It can easily overcome your senses." Her face turned serious. "Look at what happened to my poor nephew. I've seen foreigners get lost here, niños, so be careful. Temptations are strong. You must always be aware of the things you do, of persons befriending you." She looked at us thoughtfully. "But you two are strong. I can see that. You should be okay."

I glanced at Allison who gave me a puzzled shrug. I knew it was meant as a warning, a motherly advice, but I couldn't glean the full significance of it.

Later, when Señora Giron walked us to the gate, I sensed an unwillingness in her to let us go. I could only suppose she associated us with her dead nephew, some kind of a final link to what would now be a memory. I could see traces of tears brimming around her eyes.

She took Allison in her arms and hugged her like a child. "I'm glad you came, niña," the woman said. "You have no idea how good it made me feel." She looked at me soberly. "Take care of her, Jaime. You've found yourself a jewel of a woman. And don't forget to visit us sometime." With that, she turned and hurried back to the house.

As we sauntered down the hill in that bright August sunshine with our hands linked together, I could not help but feel that we had reached another plateau. We were two young lovers from faraway lands who had found each other in the most adverse circumstances. And we had prevailed. Deep in our hearts, we knew that whatever else might happen, whatever test lay before us, we would inevitably end up together. Somehow, we would find a way.

We reached the part of the trail that led to the albino's stall and saw the man whittling on a piece of wood with a pocket knife. He waved to us when we passed and said something very strange: *"Beware of the gypsy moth. Never let it between you."* Then he nodded confidently. *"Together, you will overcome it."* We were halfway down the path when a church bell sounded from the south. We both turned, my eyes looking past the mountains towards the clear blue skies beyond. Andalusia, I thought, and felt its strong pull.

"Is that where you want to go?" Allison asked. "South?"

I nodded. "Will you come with me?"

She smiled. "I'll go anywhere with you."

The End

Blue Owl Editions

To Order: Call (510) 482-3038; Email: blueowl@jps.net

You can also order THE BAND OF GYPSIES from Amazon.com and any major chain and independent bookstore. Check with the sales counter.

Please visit our webpage at http://www.jps.net/edanti for a gallery tour

Iberian Nights

Gypsy Girl With Violin

Bloodshed in the Plaza

The Bullring

Preview Excerpt

IBERIAN NIGHTS

A picaresque love story; A sensuous thriller

The adventure continues. Jaime and Allison head south, taking them to the most sensuous and agonizing experience of their lives.

Iberian Nights - Excerpt

☼ 1 The Matador's Lure

Elena lit a cigarette and cast a wild-eyed glance at the tangerine fields of New Castille, her face now bronzed from the constant sun. She was stretched out on her seat with her legs crossed, her thighs exposed. It was stifling hot. Beads of sweat glistened on her face. She caught me watching her and smiled tightly. "What's the matter querido, you like my legs?"

I shrugged. "They're nice legs," I said and closed my eyes.

Ever since we left Madrid and crossed into the ardent plains of Toledo, she had been in such an agitated state. In fact, we all were, as if the sultry nature of the land had taken over our senses. At the time, I should have taken heed of this disturbing observation, for doing so would have prepared me for the tragedy that would later befall our group.

We were on a train to Andalucia—Allison, Elena, Simone, and I—the sole remnant of that summer's exchange program which used to number twenty but had since dwindled down to four. Our other roommates had left: Bjorn had gone home to Stockholm, Cliff to London, and his lover Miguel to Caracas, to resume their former lives.

I noticed that the train had slowed down at the outskirts of some town and had just turned to my girlfriend Allison, our self-proclaimed tour director from California, when she announced, "Badajoz, the home of the cork trees."

"Cork trees?" Simone, the French girl, asked.

"Yes. According to the travel guide, it's about the only tree that grows down here."

A batch of passengers had just boarded the train, among them, a young man dressed in black with a little boy in tow. I observed the pair with interest as I found them to be incongruous with each other, for while the young man was dressed rather nattily with his flamboyant bolero jacket, black pair of pants, and black rancher's boots, the boy came in a tattered T-shirt so dirty that its color had turned from what used to be white to a sickly yellow. In fact, the poor thing didn't have any shoes on and was walking down the aisle on his bare feet.

The man gave us a perfunctory glance, stuffed his knapsack into the overhead bin, and pointed the boy to an empty seat across from us. Eying Simone, he sat down next to the boy.

I glanced at him obliquely and gauged him to be no more than thirty, although I could be wrong—Spaniards tended to look younger than their true age. He had a tan face, deep blue eyes, and sharp Spanish nose. He was not handsome by any means but quite imposing, made more so by a fervent personality that was at once apparent. "A donde vais? Where are you going?" he asked, as if it was any of his business. His eyes raked Simone.

"Sevilla," Simone said, not at all intimidated by the man.

She kicked off her shoes and wiggled her red toes, an act not lost to the Spaniard whose eyes were now riveted to her feet. Having seen her in action in Bilbao, I knew she could twist the impudent man around her little finger if she wanted to. As if to attest this point, she sparred with him easily and said, "And you, senor, where are you going?"

"Same. I have important business to attend to."

"Hmmm, what sort of business?" Simone said, not impressed.

"I'm an agent for bullfighters."

At this, all of us became attentive. "Bullfighters have agents?" Allison asked.

"Si senorita. I am a talent scout and an agent. Those I see with promise to be great matadors I take with me for training."

"Like who?" Simone said doubtfully.

"Like this little boy, senorita."

"Him? Why he is no more than ten!" Simone protested.

About the Author

Enrico Antiporda was born and raised in Manila, Philippines. He spent some time working in Spain before settling down at Oakland California where he lives with his wife. He is both a writer and a painter and has been in exhibits at galleries in the San Francisco Bay Area. The Band of Gypsies, the first of a two-book series, is his fifth novel.

Blue Owl Editions

is committed to publishing high quality paperback and artwork. It is one of the rare publishing companies offering limited edition prints and original canvases depicting the subject matter of its books. The following is a list of available limited edition prints for The Band of Gypsies and its sequel, Iberian Nights:

Gypsy Dancers I, II, and III (cover art), Iberian Nights (cover art), Gypsy Girl With Violin, Gypsy Woman (nude), The Bullring (backcover), The Bonfire, Evening On The Jetty, The Fortune Teller.